Doctor Death

A Patricia Fisher Mystery

Book 5

Steve Higgs

Text Copyright © 2019 Steven J Higgs

Publisher: Steve Higgs

The right of Steve Higgs to be identified as author of the Work has been asserted by him in accordance with the Copyright, Designs and Patents Act 1988

All rights reserved.

The book is copyright material and must not be copied, reproduced, transferred, distributed, leased, licensed or publicly performed or used in any way except as specifically permitted in writing by the publishers, as allowed under the terms and conditions under which it was purchased or as strictly permitted by applicable copyright law. Any unauthorised distribution or use of this text may be a direct infringement of the author's and publisher's rights and those responsible may be liable in law accordingly.

'Doctor Death' is a work of fiction. Names, characters, businesses, organisations, places, events and incidents either are the product of the author's imagination or are used fictitiously. Any resemblance to actual persons, living or dead, events or locations is entirely coincidental.

Dedication

To my mother – a woman who loves to cruise

Table of Contents:

- Operation Fat Wallet
- Doctor Mendoza
- Interfering Busybody
- Quarantine
- Chinese Theatre
- Ramone
- At Anchor
- The Captain
- Sick Bay
- Pick Pockets
- Telegram
- Tricky Phone Calls
- Hatching a Plot
- Agnes and Mavis
- Mr Tracksuit
- A Crazy Plan
- Day of the Living Dead
- The Brig
- Uniforms and Disguises
- Splitting the Team
- Cure
- Surrender
- What Women Can Achieve
- Dr Chouxiang
- Jermaine
- Author Note:

Extract from Murder on the Dancefloor

Clues

Operation Fat Wallet

I watched from behind wide designer sunglasses, pretending to read a magazine as I surveyed the scene and tried to keep my impatience in check. Across from me, my good friends Akamu and Rick, two senior citizens from Hawaii, were laughing raucously as they told jokes and annoyed each other.

They were at the cabana bar next to the top deck open air pool where they were supposed to be acting a little drunk. The thing is, they weren't acting anymore. At least, I didn't think they were. We set up an hour ago, just the three of us on an unsanctioned and self-appointed mission to catch a pickpocket who had been plaguing the ship for the last week.

We are passengers aboard the Aurelia, Purple Star Cruise Line's finest and most luxurious ship, and I am the guest staying in the finest suite on the whole ship. Originally intended to house royals when they came aboard, I came to be the lady in the Windsor Suite by a quirk of fate brought on by a cruel blow that turned out to be the best thing that ever happened to me. I'm Patricia Fisher, one-time wife to a philandering git and now, somehow, I am travelling the world and, while discovering myself, the tenacious woman hidden inside the bedraggled wife, I have also discovered that I am something of a sleuth.

Though I shook off my husband and have no companion with me, I am not alone; I have a butler appointed to me and have made several friends on board. Two of whom are now my accomplices as we try to solve the pickpocket case before the onboard security team can. There is no reason for my involvement, other than because I want to solve the case and catch the thief. Rick and Akamu are retired police officers; both enjoying the forgotten thrill of the chase.

Not that they will be giving chase to anyone; they are both well into their seventies and a little wobbly on their feet. Their top speed can best be described as a shuffle.

Anyway, the pickpocket has struck the bar/pool area several times in the last few days, generally picking on people with fat wallets or open handbags as they joyously pay too little attention to their belongings. That's where Rick and Akamu come in. They were drinking under the shade of the bar and making sure their wallets, bulging with notepaper not cash, were sticking out their back pockets for all to see.

Unfortunately, over an hour had slipped by and no one had tried to relieve them of their cash and cards yet. Safely tucked inside my magazine was my phone. Jermaine, my butler, had helped me construct an ingenious spy device so I could film the theft, if it occurred, while appearing to be doing nothing of the sort. Using cardboard, he reinforced the magazine to give it rigidity, then taped my phone in place so the lens looked out of the iris of the model on the front cover. It worked too. Glancing down at my magazine, I could see both men and the barman moving about behind them. The screen though was covered in dog snot, as the tiny Dachshund balanced on my lap kept nudging the screen with her nose, tracking my fingers as I zoomed in and out.

'Anna,' I said impatiently for what must have been the fiftieth time in the last hour. She inverted her head to look up at me as if I was saying her name so I could feed her a treat. When we made eye contact, I said, 'Stop touching the screen. You are making it slimy.'

She tilted her head as if trying to make sense of my words, then licked her own nose and put her head back on my lap. I tried to dry the smears from the screen with the edge of my thin sarong.

Turning my attention back to the bar, a young couple had just collected drinks and were walking away again but had not gone near either man's wallet. Just then, Rick slapped Akamu on his meaty arm and slid from his stool. I couldn't hear what he was saying but it looked like the drinks had worked their way through his system, so he was off to visit the nearest amenities.

A pair of old ladies, each of whom had to be aged somewhere around eighty, made their way to the bar. The cruise attracted a lot of retirement-aged travellers, possibly because they now had the time to indulge in the long trips or possibly because they recognised they wouldn't need to hang onto their money for much longer. Whichever the case, these two were typical passengers and I had met them in the bar a couple of days ago when we all ordered gin at the same time. They were Caucasian, with silver hair, though one had a blue rinse that contrasted with the pink cotton dress she wore to give a kind of bubble-gum effect.

As they came around Akamu, one wobbled slightly and bumped his arm, knocking his drink as he lifted it. I could see her apologising while laughing at herself, a hand to her chest to show her embarrassment.

Then, Anna growled, and I tracked her gaze to find, to my left, that a shifty-looking young man in a tracksuit and matching ballcap had appeared. Why would he be wearing a tracksuit? There was a slight breeze today which disguised the true heat, but it had to be close to one hundred degrees out of the shade. He bore all the hallmarks of a character to watch.

He was trying to look nonchalant but failing miserably, walking at an unnatural pace and looking nervous. He made a beeline for the bar, but when he got there, he didn't try to get to the bar itself. Pausing for a couple of seconds as he walked behind Akamu, and peering over his head as if looking for someone, I saw his hands move in front of his body as he did something before moving on.

With his back to me, he had effectively blocked any chance I had of filming him commit the crime but as he moved away, Akamu's back pocket was starkly bereft of his wallet and the young man had increased his pace, heading across the sun deck area to the nearest door and escape.

'Stop!' I yelled as loudly as I could. A hundred heads turned in my direction as I pointed to the young man. 'Stop him. He just stole a wallet!'

Anna barked and leapt from my lap, her lead whipping through my hands before I could get a grip on it, and she was off, sprinting across the sun deck at a speed that was frankly surprising for a dog with one-inch legs.

The man in the tracksuit and ballcap stared at her in disbelief, then started running. I was off my sun lounger but couldn't have caught the man even if I possessed superpowers. I didn't have to though. Anna was barking as she ran, attracting the attention of everyone on the sun deck; kids and parents alike were standing up or standing on their loungers to see what was happening. Akamu was up and moving too, though I passed him and left him behind as I chased my little dog.

The thief in the tracksuit was going to get away though, he had too great of a head start and was moving too fast for even Anna to catch him before he got to the nearest door and could escape her. He put his arms out to push the doors open as he got to them but glanced back at Anna as he did, so he didn't see Rick operating the storm seal latches on the other side. Rick saw the ruckus, saw the man running and me pointing and took an educated guess. The man hit the locked door at full speed; the effect much the same as running into a brick wall as he splatted against it and bounced off.

It didn't knock him out but it sure took the wind out of his sails. Dazed, he fell to the deck as a shocked gasp rippled around the crowd. The gasps, however, soon turned to cries of dismay as my untrained and disobedient dog caught up to him and bit hold of his arm.

Slipping in my elegant, expensive and completely impractical wedge-heeled shoes, there was nothing I could do to stop her. It worried me that she might hurt him and then there would be questions raised about whether she was dangerous. I was just getting used to having her around and she was so sweet, but my worries were thankfully unfounded.

The man in the tracksuit was sitting up again and had lifted his right arm into the air. Anna was hanging from it and shaking from side to side as she did her best to kill him by worrying the material of his sleeve. He uttered a few expletives and gave his arm a shake, his efforts succeeding only in making a nearby mother cover her child's ears in case he had anything else to say.

'Anna!' I shouted again, this time my voice causing the tiny dog to pause her efforts so she could peer at me even as she hung in mid-air.

Rick finally got the doors open again, but the commotion inevitably drew the attention of ship security. There were white uniforms converging on our location at speed while everyone on the sun deck was still watching us, their heads swinging about between me, the white uniforms, Mr Tracksuit, my overly aggressive dog, and the old man stumbling out through the door by the thief's feet.

Mr Tracksuit tried to get to his feet, looking around for his hat and acting a little dazed but he was quickly surrounded by security, their pace and youth getting them there at the exact same time as me.

'Put the dog down, sir,' instructed Lieutenant Baker, a tall, strong man I had come to know quite well during my time on board.

Mr Tracksuit looked up at him with a sneer. 'Put it down? Put it down? Are you kidding me? How about someone gets it off of me before I bash its head in?' I ducked between two uniforms to rescue Anna, clamping my hands around her muscular torso to pull her away though she refused to let go. Instead she continued to growl at the man and shake her head violently. 'She's ripping the material now,' he whined, getting upset.

I lowered my head so my mouth was alongside her ear. 'Come along, Anna,' I begged. 'You're making me look bad.' In the end, with the security team waiting somewhat impatiently, Rick and Akamu swaying from the alcohol, and hundreds of onlookers craning their necks for a better view, I slid my finger into the back of her mouth and prised her jaw open. She contorted her body so she could lick my face, panting from the effort and looking ever so pleased with herself.

'Thank you,' the man said, not meaning a word of it. 'Now would someone like to tell me what is going on?'

With Anna secured under one arm, I stepped forward before Lieutenant Baker or anyone else had a chance to react. 'I'll tell you what's going on. You got caught, young man. Now, hand it over, please.'

Next to me, Lieutenant Baker sighed. 'Mrs Fisher, if I might take over now.' He shot me a pair of raised eyebrows as he waited for me to step back, saying, 'Thank you,' as I acknowledged that I didn't actually have any authority here. He opened his mouth to speak to Mr Tracksuit but paused and spoke to me first. 'I must say it is so unusual to find you in the thick of it, Mrs Fisher.' His flippant comment was delivered with a smile though and I gave him an innocent face in response as if I had no idea what he was talking about.

'Hey!' said Mr Tracksuit, bringing everyone's attention back to him. 'How about someone tells me what is going on?'

This time Baker did address him, 'Sir, I must insist that you hand it over now, please.'

'Don't know what you're talking about,' Mr Tracksuit retorted.

Lieutenant Deepa Bhukari said, 'We saw you take this man's wallet.' She indicated Akamu. 'We need to escort you to a secure area for questioning and inspect your cabin for other property we believe you may have taken.'

'You didn't see me take anything,' he claimed defiantly. 'Search me. Go on. Search me,' he demanded as he lifted his arms to assume a classic pat-down pose. His confidence was worrying. Had he ditched the wallet? If so, where? I looked about to see if he had passed a trash can. His prints or DNA would be on the wallet if we found he had thrown it already. There was nothing in sight though.

Lieutenant Baker searched the man but, as expected, he found nothing. He certainly didn't find Akamu's wallet.

Wrinkling my nose, I looked back at the bar. The two old ladies were no longer there. 'Lieutenant Baker, could I have a quiet word?'

He stepped to one side with me, away from the others who were still surrounding the man in the tracksuit. We were creating a scene; more than usual I mean and would have to move away soon.

As Baker stepped close to me so I could speak quietly, I ran it through in my head again: I was about to accuse a pair of pensioners. 'There was another couple near Akamu when his wallet went missing,' I said.

Baker eyed me in confusion for a second, then said, 'You don't mean the little old ladies, do you?'

'The kid gets to lift the wallet but then palms it to one of the ladies who totters away with it in her handbag. Perfect set up.'

'No way.'

Lieutenant Baker didn't like it, but I persisted. 'The wallet has gone, Mr Tracksuit doesn't have it, and he hasn't had a chance to put it anywhere. If the ladies didn't take it, then where is it?'

His shoulders slumped in defeat. 'Okay, Mrs Fisher. Let's take a look at the lovely little old ladies.' Then he turned to the other security members just a few feet away. 'Take him to holding, please. Identify him and wait there. Mrs Fisher and I will be along soon.'

Baker started to walk away, touching my elbow gently to get me moving also. 'Just the two of us?' I asked.

'I doubt our quarry will put up much of a fight. If it's them, I will call security to join me at their cabin.' Baker was moving swiftly, walking not running but not hanging about either. He had a question for me though, 'How is it that you came to be chasing him, Mrs Fisher? It feels like too much coincidence for it to be your friend whose wallet was taken.'

'We set a trap, okay,' I admitted, setting Anna down but keeping a good hold on her lead this time as she instantly started pulling against it. 'What were you doing there?'

'It's my job,' he drawled as if he shouldn't have to remind me. 'We also had a trap set up, but I guess yours was more attractive.'

We hit the doors to go inside on the opposite side of the sun deck from where we had been. 'Do you know where you are going?' I asked.

Baker pointed down the passageway ahead of us. 'Yes, I helped the old ladies with some bags yesterday.' He fell silent for a moment though it seemed like he wanted to say something else, so I kept quiet too. Just before we reached the next corner, he said, 'Of course, I'm now wondering if the bags were theirs because there have been reports of shopping going missing.'

'Shopping?'

'Clothes. Designer goods. Some of the shops on board sell expensive items that might be attractive to a thief. I think maybe I helped them carry stolen goods to their cabin.' He said it with a sigh and as we turned the corner, we both saw the old ladies ahead of us.

They were about to get in an elevator!

'Ladies, stop!' Baker shouted, drawing the attention of everyone in sight including the old ladies. Their eyes went wide with panic, but they didn't stop as instructed. Instead, they dashed inside the elevator car, bumping into each other as they did which caused items to spill from a handbag as they desperately stabbed the button to close the doors.

Baker and I were both running, little Anna's feet skidding on the deck as she attempted to break the sound barrier while I held her in check on her lead. The doors closed before we could get there though; the faces of the two ladies looking scared as they backed against the rear wall of the car and vanished from sight.

They escaped, but not for long. Baker knew their cabin number.

On the deck by our feet were two wallets. Anna was sniffing them. 'Am I okay to pick these up?' I asked, but Baker was already on his radio, coordinating a response that would meet him at the ladies' cabin. As he did that, I knelt on the deck and fished in my own handbag for a pen.

Using it, so I didn't get my fingerprints on the wallets, I flicked them both open. Neither was Akamu's.

The first showed a Fiji address on the drivers' license in the clear plastic picture bit inside. The man was broad with an unsmiling face as one always gets with such pictures, but his age was listed as sixty-two and we had his name so the crew would be able to return his property. The second one didn't have a drivers' licence displayed inside, instead it had what looked like the identification for a doctor of some kind. It looked to be in Filipino, though there was no address shown. Scanning the details, I saw Doktor written next to the word immunology. I was willing to bet that immunology was the same word most places, so it meant exactly what I thought it meant.

'I need those, please,' said Baker, kneeling next to me to carefully scoop both wallets into two separate evidence bags using a plastic-gloved hand. 'I have a team meeting me at the ladies' cabin. It looks like another case closed.'

I went with him, though there was no need for me to do so. I like closure, I guess. Baker's confidence in closing the case was premature though because the ladies were not there when we arrived. However, the question of whether they were the thieves or not was answered unequivocally. The ladies had absconded to somewhere else on the ship and were no doubt hiding out and wondering what to do, but their cabin was filled with stolen goods. Wallets, pieces of jewellery, purses and handbags, shopping bags filled with the expensive, designer-labelled items Baker described were strewn across the bed and the chest of drawers and the dressing table and even stacked in the corners.

Lieutenant Bhukari whistled appreciatively. 'Wow. This is quite the haul. Does anyone know how long they have been on board?'

Lieutenant Pippin, another crew member I knew, answered, 'I am just looking that up now.'

Across the room, Baker was looking over the shoulders of two other men as they peered inside some of the bags. 'This is going to take a while to catalogue and return,' one said.

'We have a day,' replied Baker. 'When we dock in Phuket tomorrow, some passengers will be getting off and we need to have their belongings returned to them.'

'You're kidding right?' the man asked.

Baker eyed him curiously. 'It will take far longer if you bellyache instead of getting started.' His subordinate looked like he wanted to say something but chose instead to get on with it as suggested.

Anders spoke up to break the tension. 'The ladies got on in Singapore. They are Irish though. Their names are Agnes Eldritch and Mavis Du Maurier.' He looked up from the tablet in his hands. 'I suppose we need to circulate their pictures and find them.'

Bhukari asked, 'What do we do about the man we already took into custody?'

Baker pointed a finger at Pippin. 'Is he linked to the ladies?'

Pippin busied himself typing on the tablet, but said, 'I don't... no, not that I can see. They got on in different places, come from different countries and are staying on different decks.'

'Then we let him go and apologise,' concluded Baker. 'I'll do that myself. Pippin, get the pictures circulated to all crew and inform Commander Shriver. Bhukari, you take charge here and seal off the room.

I suggest you work quietly and with the door closed. If they cannot see anyone, the ladies may attempt to return and walk right in on top of you.'

I nodded at his plan. It was simple and might yield them an easy win. As Baker excused himself to deal with the man in the tracksuit, I realised I had no further purpose and was most likely in the way. I wasn't satisfied about Mr Tracksuit though. He had been wearing a sweat-inducing outfit in hundred-degree sunshine and there had to be a reason for that.

Checking to make sure no one was watching, I surreptitiously knocked the two wallets we found by the elevators into my handbag. Baker had placed them on the dressing table in their plastic evidence bags and they were still there, unguarded amid all the other detritus. I was going to return them, and there was more than enough evidence in the cabin to convict Agnes and Mavis, so it wasn't as if I was doing anything wrong. That's how I explained it to Anna at least.

I wanted to meet a couple of the victims; I had a few questions to ask.

Doctor Mendoza

To see if I could root out the truth about Mr Tracksuit, I first needed to obtain cabin numbers for the two men in question. I could do that back in my suite using Jermaine's login details to access central registry. I wasn't supposed to know Jermaine's login and password for the crews' onboard system of course, but he and I had come to trust each other during my time on board and there had been a few instances when we needed information to get us out of trouble.

Back in my suite, I unclipped Anna's lead and put down my handbag with the wallets inside so I could check on Jermaine. The tall Jamaican man had been at my beck and call since I came aboard the ship in Southampton and seemed to be available any time I was awake, but today, when I eyed him suspiciously and insisted he tell me the truth, he admitted that he was feeling rather under the weather. His very British phrase sounding perfectly at home in his fake Downton Abbey butler's accent, but having given up the truth, he then slumped against the counter and I helped him back through to his adjoining cabin behind my kitchen. There I demanded he lie down and rest and could tell that he was truly ill when he silently complied. I called the ship's doctor and waited an hour for him to arrive.

That it took that long was a clear indication of how many passengers and crew were coming down with something. A ship is an enclosed environment, so a cold or virus goes around fast. The doctor wasn't sure what people had but it appeared to be virulent and attacking all the body's systems at once.

I left only once Jermaine was settled, the doctor prescribed him nothing more than paracetamol. He assured me that antibiotics were not appropriate and that his two colleagues (there were three doctors on the ship) were conducting tests to work out what they were trying to treat.

My hope to find him feeling better and perhaps dusting or ironing were dashed though when I came into my living area to the sound of utter silence. I knocked gently on his door. 'Jermaine, are you in there? How are you feeling?' I called out as I pushed his door open.

From the bed came a weak reply. 'My apologies, madam, I appear to have fallen asleep. If you would be so generous as to give me a few moments, I will return to my duties.'

He was attempting to sit up in his bed. 'You'll do no such thing,' I insisted as I put a hand to his chest to arrest his movement. 'The doctor said you were to stay in bed unless absolutely necessary.' There was a sheen of sweat on his face to show the fever burning inside. 'Can I get you some water?'

As he settled back onto his pillow, I fetched a fresh pitcher and glass anyway and returned to his cabin to find Anna sitting on his chest. She wasn't making it any easier for him to breathe and was trying to nuzzle his face for affection. When I lifted her back down to the deck, he said, 'Thank you, madam.' Then added, 'I worry, madam, that I might be infectious. Perhaps it might be best if you limit your exposure.' He had a point, but I had already been exposed and felt fine so far. I didn't want to catch whatever he had but I also didn't want to leave him to fend for himself when he did so much for me. Seeing my indecision, he added, 'I plan to sleep, madam. I have everything I need.'

Seeing the sense in letting him sleep, I patted his arm and left him in the quiet and dark of his cabin. Back in my living area, I turned on the computer and poured a glass of ice water for myself. Then, eating a banana, I settled at the desk, entered Jermaine's login details and navigated to the ship's central registry where I entered the name of the man in the first wallet and then the second. On a notepad I jotted down their cabin numbers, checked on Jermaine again to confirm he was asleep and slipped quietly out of my suite to do some snooping. Anna had climbed onto a couch and was dozing. I left her there, expecting she would most likely stay put until I returned.

I had a carefree skip to my steps as I headed to the elevator bank nearest to my cabin. I was almost six weeks into my trip now, so I was half done, but I also had half left and that was reason for celebration. So many times in the past I had stared through the window of a travel agents to see the giant posters on the walls behind their desks. I had yearned to travel, but trapped inside my marriage, it had not been possible. Now I was doing it and I might just do it again some day. It was an adventure, made more so because of the occasional capers I found myself involved in and because of the impossibly handsome captain.

Captain Alistair Huntley, a handsome man with a strong body, was just over a year my senior and to all intents and purposes, we were dating. Saying it in my head put a dent in my jubilant stride though because we weren't really dating at all. He was the captain of the ship and that was his entire life. He slept, he ate, and he captained the ship. We had kissed, on several occasions now, but he wanted to keep our relationship quiet so we were not eating together in public, at least not as a couple, and we were not going to the cinema or a cabaret act or any of the things I wanted to do. As a couple at the start of things as they get to know each other, it seemed natural and normal to spend time together on typical dating activities. He was trying, I would concede that, but all too often, when we arranged dinner in my suite, he would be called away, or never even make it, calling to apologise as once again there was a matter that only he could attend to. It did not help that he was on his fourth deputy captain in five weeks, so I was making allowances for him, but I was very conscious that my time on board was limited. We either got to know each other quickly and made a decision to commit to something more, or there would be no time to do so.

Forcing away a glum frown that threatened to invade my happy face, I reached the first cabin number and fixed a smile in place as I knocked on the door. Knocking on the door at this time of day was highly speculative on my part; I thought it more likely the occupant would be out, but it wasn't far for me to go to find out. It was quiet in the passageway while I waited. The cabin was on deck eighteen and close to the stern. There was no natural light in the passageway but a blast of it hit my face as the door opened because the cabin had windows. It quickly dissipated though as the man pulled the door closed behind him leaving just a crack so he didn't need to swipe his card or knock to get back in.

Looking back at me with an annoyed expression wasn't the man in the wallet's little photo ID though. He was a shade under six feet tall and Asian by race. Though I would struggle to be accurate about his exact heritage, I wanted to say Thailand or Vietnam. I had limited experience to draw from, but his features reminded me of the people I had seen as we came though that area a few days ago. The standout feature though was his body: he was muscular. Not like a body builder, but certainly like someone who spent a lot of time in the gym lifting weights and he wore fitted clothes that made his muscular physique clear to everyone.

He didn't look friendly, but I kept my smile in place as I stated my business. 'Hello, I'm Patricia. I found this wallet and hoped I could return it to its owner. Perhaps I have the wrong cabin though.' I opened the wallet to read the name. 'I'm looking for Doctor Bayani Mendoza.'

I glanced back up just as the man reached for the wallet. 'I'll give it to him,' he said gruffly.

He was about to snatch it from my hand when I pulled it away. 'I'll give it to him in person, thank you. That way I know it went to the right person.'

His hand grabbed at thin air and now he really looked unfriendly, his forehead creasing in a deep frown as his top lip curled in a snarl. He took a step forward, but the half-closed door opened again, and a new man clamped a hand on his shoulder. 'Come now, Chai. The lady made a reasonable request.'

With another grimace in my direction, Chai disappeared back inside the room so the new man could fill the doorway. The new man looked just like the first, he might even be his older brother, but he was a couple of inches shorter just as he looked to be a couple of years older. He had the same body though: muscular and capable looking. In contrast, he had a smile fixed to his face and looked friendly, almost like someone had just told him a joke and I caught him mid laugh.

'May I see the wallet, please?' he asked. His hands were behind his back and showing no sign that they might try to grab for it as the last man had.

'Of course.' I held it up and open for him to see. As he leaned in, I said, 'Is your brother alright? He seemed upset.'

The man was leaning forward to inspect the tiny picture but shifted his eyes up at my question to look directly at me. Then he straightened, a guarded expression now dominating his features. 'You are very perceptive, Mrs...'

'Fisher. Patricia Fisher.' I brought the hand with the wallet down as I lifted my other hand to shake. 'I think most people would be able to identify you are brothers. You look very alike.'

He simply nodded. 'Doctor Mendoza is inside; I will fetch him if you give me a moment.'

He was polite about it, but he still closed the door in my face as he moved away. Perhaps they were doing something private or maybe someone was getting changed. I didn't want to speculate but it was clear they didn't want me to see inside.

Voices coming from inside were muffled but still sounded like they were arguing. I tried to make out what was being said, though I refrained from placing my ear against the door. Telling myself they were probably speaking in a language I didn't know, I let it pass but I was made to wait as if Doctor Mendoza was too busy to retrieve his wallet.

By the time the door opened again more than two minutes later, I was bored and getting quite peeved, my attitude held in check only by reminding myself that I wouldn't have to wait if I kept my nose out. Nevertheless, I could hear a touch of impatience in my voice when a man resembling the one in the wallet I held, finally came to the door.

'Doctor Mendoza? Thank you for finding the time to see me. I believe this is yours.' I handed him the wallet with it open to reveal his picture. 'I was able to retrieve this during a sting operation earlier today. Can I ask you a few questions?' Okay, I was stretching the truth and making myself sound like a special forces detective or something, but I had come this far and I wanted to get a couple of answers. Doctor Mendoza risked a glance behind him at the door and I dropped my attitude as I realised how nervous he looked. Now what had I stumbled across? 'Is everything okay?' I asked, my voice a hushed breath.

He stared at me and swallowed, blinking rapidly. 'Yes. Yes, of course. I hadn't noticed my wallet was missing actually. I can't imagine how I managed to drop it.'

He continued to blink at me, far more rapidly and frequently than could be natural. My brain told me he was trying to convey something that he couldn't say, but I wasn't getting the message yet. I decided to keep him talking.

'Actually, you were probably robbed. There has been a team of pickpockets operating on board for the last few days. Can I ask you to look at someone and...?'

'Doctor Mendoza,' a voice came from inside. It was the older brother I determined from the calm tone the voice carried. 'Time is of the essence. We must press on.'

The doctor cast his eyes down at the deck, his shoulders slumping in defeat and when he looked back up, he looked wretched. I had seen a look like this before, on the face of Riku Takahashi just before he jumped from the back of the ship. My heart caught in my throat as he looked into my eyes.

'I must go, I'm afraid.' He made to move back through the door, but I grabbed his arm. I wanted answers about Mr Tracksuit, but right now I was just using that as an excuse to keep his attention. 'I need you to look at a short piece of video, Dr Mendoza. It will take just a few seconds.'

'Doctor Mendoza,' the voice from inside said again, this time with more insistence in it.

'I really must go,' he apologised. 'Our work really is time sensitive.'

'What are you working on,' I tried, but my question bounced off a closed door as the man slipped back inside and closed the door. It was incredibly rude, but I wasn't angry or offended; I was curious. There was something going on here and I needed help to find out what. My gut told me Doctor Mendoza was in some kind of trouble though I had no idea what kind of trouble it might be. Perhaps Alistair would be able to help me.

I wriggled my nose a little as I continued to stare at the closed door. When he slipped back through it, I got a very brief glance inside. The room was filled with laboratory equipment; a centrifuge, some kind of analysing equipment and a host of other items I couldn't identify but which looked like high-tech medical gear. It had only been a brief glance, but the contents of the room were not normal for people on a cruise plus the doctor had been very nervous.

Leaving the issue to stew in my head for a while, I walked away, taking myself to the cabin of the other man whose wallet I held. In contrast to Doctor Mendoza, the owner was overjoyed to get it back. Where Doctor Mendoza hadn't even thanked me, Semi Batiluna tried to give me all the cash in his wallet as a reward for returning it and I had to fight off the offer of dinner and cocktails which he insisted upon several times in a bid to wear me down. I showed him the footage I had of Mr Tracksuit, but he didn't recognise him. It was a dead end this time, but it wasn't enough to put me off.

In the end, the excited Mr Batiluna settled for a handshake but tricked me and pulled me into a hug which his wife then joined. Walking back to my suite, I felt buoyant, but where my thoughts had been filled with the idea that I might prove Mr Tracksuit was involved, now I couldn't shift the belief that Doctor Mendoza was in trouble and I was going to have to be the one to see he got help.

It was time to interfere.

Interfering Busybody

I didn't know the young lieutenant I was addressing, and it was clear he didn't know me either. It was one of the problems with the Aurelia being so big: there were too many crew for one to get to know more than a handful of them. Making a beeline for the elevator entrance to the bridge, I knew I couldn't access it, but hoped I would be able to find one of the crew I did know and be able to speak with Commander Shriver or the captain through them.

They would both take my concerns seriously enough that they would send security to check on the doctor's wellbeing. The young man barring my path was making my mission difficult though.

'I'm sorry, madam, the bridge cannot be accessed by the guests,' he said for the second time.

'Yes, I know that. I don't need to go myself; I just need you to use your radio to contact Commander Shriver so that she will come down.'

'Commander Shriver will not take kindly to be disturbed by trivial matters, madam. If you have concerns about another guest, the correct approach is to discuss it with guest services.'

My next sentence died on my lips as I recognised the futility of presenting a new argument. I reached into my handbag and produced my phone instead. Holding it up, I pressed the screen and selected the right number to call. The young lieutenant wanted to call the elevator and get on board but was waiting for me to move away so I wouldn't try something daft like forcing my way on with him.

As the call connected, I gave him a smile, 'Alistair, hello, yes. I'm very well thank you. I hoped I might be able to steal a few moments of your time. Or Commander Shriver's. Yes. Urgent? Probably not, but I am concerned about a guest and... well, let's just say my nose is itching.' I listened for a few more seconds, then said goodbye and disconnected. 'Commander Shriver is on her way down,' I told the young lieutenant.

His face was a picture of disbelief. 'Did you just phone the captain? How is it that you have his number? No one has his number.'

I shrugged and smiled sweetly, obeying Alistair's request that we keep our relationship under wraps. It was quiet enough in the passageway for us to hear the elevator approaching from above so I took a step back and waited for the door to open, the androgynous form of Commander Shriver filling the doorway as the car opened. Flanking her, one to each side, were two more members of crew in white uniform.

She nodded in my direction as she stepped out. 'Mrs Fisher. You have something that demands my attention?'

Still staring opened-mouthed at me, the young lieutenant got into the lift as I turned away. I frowned at myself as I worked out what I wanted to say. What exactly had I seen? 'I visited a man this afternoon when I found his wallet.' I didn't expand on where I had found it. 'He had at least two other men in his cabin and he seemed very nervous... agitated even and when I glanced inside, the cabin was filled with laboratory equipment.'

'Laboratory equipment?' she echoed.

'Oh, I should have said that he is a doctor. The man whose wallet I found that is. I can't say what profession the other chaps might be but they didn't look like doctors.'

'What did they look like?' she asked. We reached an elevator bank, the commander patiently letting me lead her without explaining where we were going.

I pressed the button to summon the car then answered her question. 'Like special forces soldiers.' Her expression told me I needed to expand on my description. 'They had that well-trained, dangerous look about them. Like they are very serious people and not to be underestimated. Wired up tight, does that make sense?'

A ping signalled the arrival of the elevator and conversation stopped as we joined a dozen passengers inside. Getting off at eighteen, Commander Shriver briefed her men before following me. 'Hunt, Wong, I want you both to wait out of sight; this could be nothing so I have no desire to startle the guests by appearing in force. I will approach alone, Mrs Fisher,' she said, turning to me. 'I will advise them that there had been a noise complaint and ask to see inside their cabin. If I see anything that worries me, I will call Hunt and Wong forward. You should remain out of sight.'

I nodded at her plan. If there was something going on, she would be able to return with the right number of people, but she would have two armed men waiting out of sight if the occupants were up to something and turned hostile.

As requested, I hid around the corner. She had the cabin number so as we came into the passageway I held back and let her perform her job. I couldn't now say what it was that I expected to happen, but what did happen wasn't it.

From my position at the end of the passageway, I watched Commander Shriver rap her knuckles smartly on the door three times and wait, standing crisply at ease. The door opened a few seconds later though with a burst of music escaping. It sounded like there was party going on inside. Then a face appeared. Peering around the corner as I was, I couldn't make out who had come to the door, but when he spoke, I determined that it was the older brother; the calm one.

'Hey, how you doing?' asked a slurring voice. Then I saw it was the older brother from earlier as he stumbled into the passageway having lost his balance slightly.

He was drunk? How the heck was he drunk? He had changed his clothing too. Wearing a pair of knee-length pink shorts and a garish Hawaiian shirt, he looked completely different.

He almost bumped into Commander Shriver, her hands coming up to catch his shoulders as he caught his balance again. He was in the passageway now but turned to his cabin. 'Hey, did anyone order a stripper?' he called with a laugh. 'I got one here, but she's not very pretty.'

Wong was positioned a few feet in front of me and had sniggered at the man's first comment then winced at the second as if expecting violence to follow the insult.

Commander Shriver ignored his jibe though, peering around him to look inside the cabin. Light was pouring out of the open door to illuminate her. Whatever they were trying to hide before was now on full display and my curiosity was too great to keep me in place any longer.

'Mrs Fisher,' hissed Lieutenant Wong as I passed him. It wasn't the plan, but I wanted to see inside. Before I got to the door, Commander Shriver went through it, following the drunk man as he disappeared from sight.

I could hear her explaining her presence, the lie about a noise complaint now far more believable. The music dipped in volume just as I got to the room, someone turning it down, no doubt, but the door was open this time to reveal the laboratory equipment I saw earlier.

On almost every surface and on a pair of fold out tables, was an array of high-tech equipment with brand names I didn't recognise though they all read something instruments or a derivative thereof. None of it was doing anything. Which is to say that the centrifuge wasn't whirring and the digital readouts, on those items that had one, were all blank. In the middle of the room was another table, but there was no equipment on it; they were playing cards.

The brothers I met earlier were accompanied by two women that appeared to be racially similar so could be wives or sisters and a fifth man of the same race was in the background, making drinks. They were all dressed for Mardi-Gras wearing silly necklaces and party hats or fake glasses in gaudy colours. Empty bottles of rum were stacked next to the sink in the small kitchen area. Doctor Mendoza sat at the table with cards in his left hand and a half empty glass by his right.

I didn't know what to say. Commander Shriver did though. 'It seems we have interrupted your game. Before we go, can I ask what all the equipment is for?'

The elder brother answered, 'We are all doctors. We work in the field of infectious diseases and specialise in the testing of new equipment. It's very lucrative,' he added.

Then one of the women spoke, 'Tien, don't brag. It's impolite,' she chided.

'Sorry,' he apologised to her and then again to us. 'Sorry. That was rude of me. We are on our way home from the Philippines having just secured a major new deal and we felt like celebrating.'

Commander Shriver accepted the explanation with a nod. 'I'm glad you are enjoying your time on board the Aurelia. It is our sole desire to make your stay as perfect as possible. If there is anything the crew can do for you, please do not hesitate to call guest services.' She backed toward the door, turning to usher me out as she got close. 'Come along, Mrs Fisher. We are done here.'

'But...'

'We are done here,' she insisted. Doctor Mendoza didn't look up once, focusing intently on the table and his hand of cards. All was not okay, but I couldn't identify what it was that was wrong, not in time for me to get Commander Shriver to do anything about it anyway.

With the door shut and the relative quiet of the passageway returning, I felt like an interfering busybody with all the negative attributes such a term suggested. Commander Shriver was looking at me as if she wanted an apology for her wasted time, but she was going to have a long wait for that. Something was happening here, something bad, and I was the only one that knew about it.

'They are definitely up to something,' I stated, standing fast in the passageway while the others clearly wanted to move on. 'I disturbed them earlier, interrupting what they were doing, and they realised their behaviour was odd enough to attract attention. When I left, they changed the room around in case someone else came snooping.'

Wong and Hunt were quiet, but I could see the disbelief in their faces. Commander Shriver was equally sceptical. 'Mrs Fisher, why would they do that? What on earth can they be up to that requires such levels of subterfuge?'

'Isn't that exactly the question?' I replied as if she was completely on side and had raised the question to be helpful. She wasn't though and I was going to have a tough sell to get her to help me. 'Look, you have to decide if you believe it normal for a team of doctors to bring laboratory equipment onboard a cruise ship.'

Commander Shriver frowned and sighed. The two of us were not friends, but we were not adversaries either. There was mutual respect, I believed, but I could see she wasn't going to assist me. 'Mrs Fisher, I want you to see this from my perspective. The good doctor and his companions offered a rational and reasonable explanation for the laboratory equipment, they are acting just like passengers on a cruise and I need you to focus on that very important word: Passengers. They are passengers that have paid for passage and they are not visibly doing anything wrong. Despite what you might have seen earlier, I have no grounds to conduct a search of their cabin.'

'Cabins.'

'I'm sorry?'

'Cabins. There were four men and two women in a cabin designed to house two people and perhaps a child. They have more than one cabin so could be doing goodness knows what in the other cabins.'

Commander Shriver nodded to acknowledge the point, but said, 'Nevertheless, I have no grounds to conduct a search and I must warn you, Mrs Fisher, your... friendship with the captain notwithstanding, I shall take a dim view if I discover you have disguised yourself as a cleaner to gain entry to anyone's cabin.' My face coloured as I remembered getting caught during that caper and that Commander Shriver saw me in my hashed cleaner's outfit.

She shifted her gaze to look at her two subordinates. 'I think that will conclude this outing. Return to your stations.' Then she fixed her gaze back on me, offering a pleasant smile. 'Good day, Mrs Fisher.'

I stared at her back as she walked away, remaining in place while I considered my next move. What did I actually know? I thought about the answer to that question as I began to drift back to my suite. By the time I pulled my keycard from the handbag, the only conclusion I could draw was that I knew nothing. I met a man that seemed lost. Hopelessly lost, and there was something very strange about his relationship with the other people in his cabin. Considering it now, I wanted to say that they were controlling him. The way they reminded him he had work to do; the tone employed made it sound like they held some kind of hold over him.

I would have a chat with Rick and Akamu over dinner later. We had a table booked in General Tso's Chinese Fantasy, a restaurant on the seventeenth deck that also put on a show. I had wanted to go for some time, but the show wasn't on every night and I refused to go by myself. Going tonight only occurred to me when Jermaine fell ill and couldn't make dinner.

Remembering Jermaine quickened my pace as I hurried through the door to check on him. Anna, not one to expend unnecessary energy, opened a single eyelid as I crossed the room, but closed it again after I cooed at her. Having never owned a dog before, I wasn't sure what to expect but anecdotes and the television made me believe that a dog was supposed to leap from its bed when the master or mistress returned. If so, then Anna elected to defy modern convention, acting as if she and I were on equal terms.

Leaving her to it, I knocked again on Jermaine's door, quietly so I might not rouse him if asleep but loud enough to announce my presence if he happened to be awake. I got no response so with equal stealth, I let myself in.

He appeared to be asleep. His water was largely untouched, and the same sheen of sweat was visible on his skin. I bit my lip while I deliberated what to do, but soon decided he might benefit from eating plus I wanted to get some water in him; Dr Kim said he needed to keep taking fluids.

'Jermaine,' I called using a volume that should have been enough to wake him. 'Jermaine,' again when he failed to respond the first time. He really was in a deep sleep. Touching his arm achieved the same effect so I grabbed his shoulder and gave him a shake and it was at this point that I started to worry. Using increasing volume and force, I couldn't wake him; he wasn't asleep, he was unconscious.

Flustered with panic, I returned to my living area, leaving the door to his cabin open so I would hear him if he did wake up. Glancing back at him once more, I snatched up the phone and dialled three digits for the onboard medical emergency response.

When a voice answered, I didn't give them much chance to speak before I launched into my plea for help. 'This is Patricia Fisher in the Windsor suite. My butler was seen by Dr Kim this morning. He has been running a fever for several hours and has lost consciousness. I repeat; he is unconscious. I cannot get him to wake up. His pulse is fast, his breathing is slow, and he is sweating profusely.'

The person at the other end let me finish but didn't speak immediately as if still writing notes. Then I heard a muffled exchange as if two people were speaking but a hand was over the mouthpiece. I couldn't hear much but it sounded like one of them said, 'Another one.'

'Dr Kim will be with you shortly. Please do not touch the patient, Mrs Fisher. This is very important. He may be infectious.' I looked down at my hand; it had Jermaine's sweat on it still. Washing it off had been second to getting the doctor on my list of tasks.

The phone went back in its cradle and I found myself staring at my hands. I wanted to wash them, but I also wanted to return to Jermaine despite the warning I just heard. If he was infectious, surely I had already exposed myself. I deliberated for a few seconds, but hygiene won so I cleaned my hands at the kitchen sink using soap and water, then went to my bedroom where I searched until I found a handbag sized bottle of antibacterial gel. I knew I had one, but it took a minute to locate it.

Then, with my hands clean, I went back to check on Jermaine. Anna's eyes opening each time I crossed the room though the lazy Dachshund saw no reason to move.

It was more than half an hour before the doctor arrived, my time spent sitting on a dining table chair next to Jermaine's bed where I could monitor him and be able to accurately report his condition. The doctor's arrival was announced by Anna as she leapt from the couch already barking before she hit the floor. I wasn't fast enough to do anything about her and learned in my first couple of days with her, how futile asking her to desist was.

By the time I reached the door, her nose was pressed into the tiny gap at the bottom where she alternately sniffed for evil on the other side and barked/growled her warning that anyone entering was likely to suffer Dachshund death.

I scooped her up to tuck her under my left arm as I opened the door and started to speak before I even saw who was outside, 'Thank you for…' However, when the doctor pushed passed me and was followed by two orderlies pushing a hospital bed, my polite greeting to thank him for his speedy response, died on my lips. They were hurrying through the suite, heading for the kitchen and Jermaine's apartment and they were all wearing face masks.

'Dr Kim,' I called out as I rushed after them. 'Dr Kim, whatever is going on?'

'Stand back please, Mrs Fisher. We need to take your butler into quarantine, I'm afraid,' he replied without looking at me, setting his bag down and performing checks on the patient instead while the orderlies set up the bed behind him.

Gripped with real concern now, something I had been able to keep at bay by telling myself I was overreacting, I asked, 'What is it?'

Dr Kim was on his knees using a thermometer in Jermaine's ear to record his temperature. Looking over his shoulder I saw the number pop up: 104.8. His fever was worse than any I had experienced or witnessed. The doctor pushed off the floor to allow the orderlies room and stepped out of the way and into my kitchen as he pulled off his mask. 'These things are useless anyway,' he remarked as he discarded it. 'To answer your question, I don't know what it is. What I do know is that I now have forty-seven patients, mostly passengers but some crew, all displaying the same symptoms. Your butler is the twelfth to lose consciousness, but I suspect all are heading that way. Loss of consciousness appears to occur roughly thirty-six hours after the first symptoms present. I have an old couple and a young girl that I am quite concerned about.' I had my hand to my face as I listened. The ship was gripped by an unknown infection that was causing a level of sickness the doctor felt concerning and Jermaine was among the infected.

'Is he going to be alright?' I asked, my voice filled with trepidation for the answer.

Dr Kim pursed his lips and huffed. In Jermaine's cabin, the two orderlies were carefully manoeuvring the tall Jamaican man onto the bed, no easy task in the confined space given his size and that he had to weigh more than two-hundred pounds. 'I don't know,' the doctor finally admitted. 'There might be no reason to worry, but I am not yet sure what I am treating, and the patients are not responding to anything I give them. Of course, this is a cruise ship, so I don't have complex medicine to offer them. I need the captain to get us to a port where they can be transferred to a proper facility and have access to an immunology team.'

A light pinged on inside my head. 'There's an immunologist on board. I met him earlier.'

'There is?'

I nodded vigorously. 'Yes. Dr Benyani Mendoza.' I didn't bother to explain how I came to meet him or my concern for his companions; it was unimportant now.

'Benyani Mendoza,' Dr Kim repeated. 'Benyani Mendoza is on board this ship right now?'

'Yes. Do you know him?'

Dr Kim had the look of a man who had just been thrown a lifeline and was trying to cling to it in a stormy sea. 'I attended a lecture he gave in Seattle a few years ago. He is an expert in his field and was awarded the Nobel Prize for Medicine five years ago. I don't know him personally, but if he is on board, I need to speak with him right now.'

The orderlies were standing by the hospital bed, one at each end with Jermaine between them and securely strapped to it. He looked asleep and I wished that were the case.

'Take him to quarantine. I'll meet you there.' Dr Kim sent the orderlies on their way, holding the door to Jermaine's cabin open so they could leave, then gathered his things. 'You said you met him; do you know where he is staying?'

'I do actually,' I admitted. I could simply give the doctor the cabin number and let him get on with it, but I had legitimate reason to go snooping again now. Ha! Take that Commander Shriver. No dressing up required. I was going back to see the dangerous-looking brothers again and this time I felt certain he was going to leave his chaperones/guards/whatever they were behind so I could ask him what was going on.

    Patricia the sleuth rides again!

Quarantine

'Patty, what's going on?' the familiar voice of my gym instructor friend Barbie came from behind me as I followed Dr Kim. I turned to see her jogging toward me along the passageway. 'I just saw Jermaine on a hospital bed, but they wouldn't let me go with him. What's going on?' she repeated.

We were heading for the elevators, Barbie quickly closing the distance and slowing her pace to walk with us. 'There is some kind of infectious disease on board. People are getting sick.'

'Shhh,' insisted Dr Kim, putting a finger to his lips as we neared other passengers at the elevator. 'There is no reason for people to panic, but that doesn't mean they won't. In this kind of enclosed environment, it's quite possible that everyone on board is already exposed. Until I can identify what it is and begin treating it, I cannot accurately tell anyone what symptoms to look for or what course of action to take. In the absence of that information, it is best to keep everyone in the dark for as long as we can.'

'Won't they find out anyway?' I asked. 'People are getting sick.'

Dr Kim shook his head. 'Not in large enough numbers for it to be noticed. Not yet anyway.'

Lowering my voice, I turned back to Barbie. 'I am taking Dr Kim to meet another doctor. There is a team on board that specialises in this sort of problem. They might be able to help out.' As we reached the elevator and the small crowd gathered there, we all fell quiet.

'How are the allergy shots working out for you?' Dr Kim asked Barbie as the elevator doors closed.

She smiled her infectious smile back at him. 'Really good thank you. Patricia's little doggy hasn't made me sneeze once yet.'

Dr Kim nodded in acknowledgement but had nothing else to say. Minutes later, and for the third time in less than two hours, I was standing outside Dr Mendoza's cabin. I deffered to Dr Kim though, standing to one side so he could be the one knocking on the door. Barbie was next to me, nervous energy radiating from her as she worried about her friend.

When the door opened, it was Tien that answered once more, but his secretive behaviour had returned; the door closing quickly behind him so we couldn't see into the room. 'Can I help you?' he asked, seeing Dr Kim first. A frown briefly crinkled his forehead as he saw me again, but it was gone as soon as it appeared.

'I'm Dr Hanso Kim. I'm hoping to find Dr Benyani Mendoza. I heard him speak at a conference a few years ago and we exchanged emails. I am the senior physician on board the Aurelia and I believe I need his help.' When Tien didn't reply immediately, Dr Kim asked, 'Can we come in? It is quite urgent.'

'Who is it?' asked Dr Mendoza's voice from behind the closed door.

A grimace creased Tien's face, but he forced it away and extended his hand. 'Good day, Dr Kim. I'm Dr Tien Chouxiang. I am a colleague of Dr Mendoza's. Won't you please come in and we shall see how we can help you?'

With a quick back heel, the door opened behind him to once again reveal the cabin full of laboratory equipment. The card table was gone along with the rum and the gaudy outfits they had worn earlier. The equipment was still not being used but Dr Mendoza bore a guilty expression.

What were they up to? And better yet, why weren't they drunk anymore? I didn't ask the question. I just filed it away for later.

Dr Kim recognised the immunologist, advancing across the room to shake his hand. 'Dr Mendoza, so nice to meet you in person. I need to commend you for your work in disease control.'

Dr Mendoza, if anything, looked taken aback by the compliment. His hand came up automatically in response to Dr Kim offering his, but it was now hanging limply in Dr Kim's grip as Dr Mendoza thought of something to say. 'Thank you,' he managed weakly. He didn't need to say anything else though because Dr Kim was talking again.

'I'm sure you are here on vacation, but I really need your help in identifying a viral disease that is spreading through the ship. It is presenting initially like influenza, but the symptoms quickly develop to something more closely resembling malaria. I did some work in Zaire years ago so have experienced malaria first-hand many times. After a period of little more than twenty-four hours after first presentation, during which headaches, stomach cramps and a very high fever also present, patients begin to lose consciousness. I have more cases being reported every hour. It feels like your presence here was ordained by God himself.' Dr Kim was already moving toward the door, clearly intent on taking the immunologist to the sick bay straight away. When Dr Mendoza didn't move, he said, 'Is there something wrong, doctor? I need your help to identify this disease so I can arrange for treatment. At the rate we are going, the whole ship will be sick by tomorrow afternoon.'

Dr Mendoza appeared conflicted. Dr Chouxiang spoke up instead, 'Dr Mendoza, we really must give our assistance. There may be lives at stake.'

'Yes. Yes, of course,' said Dr Mendoza finally waking up it seemed. 'Lead on, please.'

Dr Kim wasted no time on getting back out the door to head in the direction of sickbay. In the cabin, as Barbie and I filed back outside, the two Dr Chouxiangs and Dr Mendoza had a hushed conversation in a huddle. I couldn't hear what they were saying but when they broke, I saw the grimace on Dr Mendoza's face. I told myself it could mean anything, but whatever it was, it wasn't something positive.

They collected medical bags and followed Dr Kim, Barbie and I trailing along silently behind them. In the lead, Dr Kim continued to chatter in medical terms, explaining nothing to the thickies at the back so I was instantly lost in a jungle of medical jargon and long words that all sounded likely to kill a person if left untreated.

There were numerous medical facilities on board the ship, a first aid station on every deck at least, but the medical facility Dr Kim took us to was on the sixth deck, out of the way of regular passengers as its location was on the top deck of the crew only area. It looked like a small hospital ward. There were different sections beyond the woman on reception and an operating theatre, no doubt for performing minor surgeries when the ship was crossing an ocean and couldn't put into port for a few days. The double doors leading to the ward had a hastily erected sign on them saying quarantine – obey universal precautions.

I didn't know what universal precautions were, but Dr Kim began handing out over-boots, little plastic slip on things that went over our shoes as well as facemasks with filters and gloves. 'I'm sorry we do not have better protective equipment. This is just a basic medical facility, able to deal with cuts and broken bones and perhaps an accidental amputation or appendicitis. This though,' he indicated the ward we were about to enter, 'is something we never anticipated.'

Barbie touched my arm. 'Patty is this safe? For us, I mean. Are we safe to go in there?'

I had not thought to question it. 'I'm going in,' I replied. 'There's something fishy about the Drs Chouxiang and their other colleagues. Besides, I have been touching Jermaine and if Dr Kim is right, there won't be a safe place on the ship to hide from the virus. If you haven't been exposed yet, maybe you should wait out here,' I suggested. I could see her tussling with making the right decision, so I made it for her, leaving her behind as I followed the doctors into the quarantine area.

The beds were full. The double doors led to a wide corridor from which a dozen doors led to private rooms in which patients could be housed if their condition was such that they couldn't return to their cabins. I wondered if the rooms had ever been full before because they had to be full now; I could see another dozen patients lining the corridor on makeshift beds. Ahead of me, Dr Kim explained that the crew were working on making a larger facility in one of the storerooms.

Another doctor, a woman I recognised, came out of one of the private rooms as she heard us approach. 'Dr Kim, when the orderlies brought in the latest patient without you, I worried you had been called away to treat someone else.'

'Not this time, Dr DuPont, but I don't suppose it will be long before we get more calls.'

'Well, they had better get on with converting that storeroom then because we have no room left here.'

The elder Dr Chouxiang stopped as he reached the first patient. She was a middle-aged woman who looked a bit like me: a few pounds overweight, blond hair and average height. She was unconscious, that much was evident, but it was her skin that worried me most, it looked waxy and bruised.

Dr Kim stopped next to him. 'She has worsened in the last hour. What do you make of the subcutaneous haemorrhaging?' he asked.

'Um, Dr Mendoza,' Dr Chouxiang deferred. 'This is more your area of expertise.'

Dr Kim blushed. 'I'm sorry. I thought you were all immunologists.'

'Yes. Yes, we are,' replied Dr Chouxiang defensively as if taking offense. 'Dr Mendoza is more familiar with Ebola than either myself or my brother.'

'Ebola?' echoed Dr Kim in a way that terrified me. 'You think this is Ebola?'

Now it was Dr Chouxiang's turn to blush. 'I, um… that is… isn't it obvious? The presentation is classic.'

'Hardly,' argued Dr Kim. 'Ebola's final stages may involve haemorrhaging, but it takes twenty days or more to reach that stage, not less than forty-eight hours.'

'What Dr Chouxiang means,' said Dr Mendoza, speaking for the first time but looking utterly morose, 'is that the symptoms he can see, are more closely aligned with the Ebola virus than any other known disease. Isn't that right, Dr Chouxiang?'

'Yes, of course that's what I meant.'

'Where is Special Rating Clarke, please,' I asked. I couldn't do anything for him, but I wanted to see him anyway.

It was Dr DuPont that answered. 'I have just been settling him with the nurse. Is he your butler?' she asked.

'Yes. Is he in there?' I pointed to the room she had just left, thinking it strange he would get a room when there were already people lining the corridor but soon discovered that the room had three patients in it, two of whom were on mattresses on the floor. His face was still covered in a light sheen of sweat from the fever and he looked pale. A drip was hooked up to his right forearm via an IV line, delivering fluids since they had no drugs to give him. Dr Kim's face appeared around the door frame. 'What will it mean if this is Ebola?' I asked him, going for the direct question.

'I don't think there is any need to jump to conclusions over the diagnosis yet, Mrs Fisher. The doctors and I will conduct some tests and see what we can conclude. At this time, the patients are resting and comfortable. Thank you for guiding me to Dr Mendoza, but I must insist that you get clear of the quarantine area now. Please report immediately if you begin to feel in any way unwell.'

I wanted to argue and stay with Jermaine just so I could keep an eye on the Drs Tien and Chai Chouxiang, but I sensed there was no argument I could present that would achieve that result. With a final pat on Jermaine's arm, I straightened and left the room. 'You will let me know if his condition deteriorates, won't you, Dr Kim?'

'Of course, Mrs Fisher.'

I left him then, heading back out through the ward doors to find Barbie nervously pacing where I left her. A nurse stopped me as I came through the first set of doors. I needed to shuck my mask, gown and booties at this point before proceeding outside.

Barbie watched me through the plastic curtain. 'How is he?' she asked the moment I came out. 'How is anyone?'

'They are sick and so is Jermaine. It's some kind of viral disease and looks quite nasty.'

'Is he going to be okay?' she asked, peering through the doors in the hope she might see him.

I didn't know how to answer that. Dr Chouxiang named a disease I knew to have a high mortality rate and he had seemed to know what it was just by looking at one patient. Whether he was right, or Dr Kim was, I couldn't tell. There was something very odd going on, but as I began walking away, I had to acknowledge that I didn't have any idea what it was.

Chinese Theatre

Against my better judgement, I decided to go out for dinner with Rick and Akamu as planned. My decision was based mostly on the belief that I would go stir-crazy in my suite by myself because I would do nothing but worry about Jermaine.

On the way down to the chaps' cabin, I didn't see anyone looking ill or pass by orderlies carrying a patient on a stretcher and there was no announcement given over the ship's tannoy at any point warning people to look out for the symptoms in themselves and others. Maybe it was to be a small and isolated problem and the patients would all recover now that Dr Mendoza and his team were assisting. If other people were getting sick still, there was no sign of it.

Nevertheless, the odd behaviour of the immunologists had set me on high alert, and it took a little while and a gin and tonic before I began to feel myself relaxing. The food was excellent, which came as no surprise; I hadn't had a bad meal since I came on board. It was plentiful too, the waiters continually circulating with different dishes for us to select from. I stopped only when I could feel my hold-it-all-in knickers getting tight but Rick and Akamu continued to indulge until they were fit to burst.

The evening was divided into two halves: food first and entertainment second. During the meal, a singer provided music but once the tables were cleared, the curtains on the stage opened to reveal a pair of men with large drums hung in front of them on a frame. They started thumping out a beat and soon other percussion instruments began mixing in with them. Then two duelling dragons in traditional Chinese costumes appeared from either side of the room.

I think there was a story to go with it because a young woman dressed as an innocent maiden had to be rescued by a man on a cardboard horse at one point. I struggled to follow it and struggled to keep my concentration on anything other than the strange doctors and the worrying disease I knew to be endangering every person on board.

As the applause died, I had to stifle a yawn. As usual, my routine saw me in the gym this morning just after six o'clock, so I was getting tired now that it was after ten. I had never been much of a night owl, but far less so now that I was rising early each day. 'Would either of you gentlemen like a nightcap?' I asked. I could make myself a gin and tonic in my suite but not having Jermaine there to make it for the first time since I came on board would make me feel his absence more keenly. I was going to miss him when the Aurelia finally arrived back in Southampton and I had to leave. 'I'm getting a gin and tonic,' I announced as I stood up. 'Can I get you one too?'

Both men thanked me kindly and ordered bourbon over ice, Rick pointing out that gin was an old ladies drink. I left them chatting while I went to the bar. Unusually, I had to wait a while as the one barman in sight was rushed off his feet trying to deal with all the people wanting drinks. It gave me time to check my phone for messages. Of course, I was hoping to see something from Alistair, but the stupid device was somehow blocking what he surely must be sending me. I hadn't seen him since yesterday even though we had spoken briefly this afternoon when I wanted Commander Shriver's help.

Jamming the phone back into my bag with a grumpy snarl, I saw it was my turn to be served. In contrast to the all-Chinese staff working the stage show and waiting the tables, the man behind the bar appeared to be Indian. Better yet, he had a Glaswegian accent when he spoke. 'What can I get you, madam?'

'I'll have two glasses of bourbon over ice and one gin and tonic, please. I'll take the Hendricks, please,' I added, seeing it lurking between the other bottles.

'Sorry, madam. We are out of tonic.' I stared at him for a second, waiting for him to say he was only joking. He didn't though, but he did feel the need to expand. 'Our store is empty. An issue with stocktaking, I think. I'm sure it was there when I checked yesterday, but when I sent for more earlier, the other barman came back empty handed. He's looking for more now.'

Well that explained why there was only one man behind the bar and customers waiting to be served. It didn't explain the lack of tonic though. 'Are you telling me that the tonic, just the tonic specifically, had gone missing from your store.'

'Yes. Would you still like the bourbons? I can mix you a gin fizz or a gimlet instead, madam. On the house for your disappointment.'

I puckered my lips in annoyance. It wasn't the man's fault but now I had to get a drink I didn't want and be polite about it. 'I'll have the gin fizz please. That sounds delightful.' As I watched him make it, I quickly decided it didn't look delightful at all. It had a raw egg white in it for starters. In went fresh lemon juice, sugar syrup, ice and gin which was shaken vigorously and poured over ice. Then he topped it off with soda water and added a cherry. The finished article looked okay, I guess. I swiped my card, collected the glasses and made my way back to the table.

'What's that?' asked Rick. 'It don't look like no gin and tonic to me.'

Frowning, I said, 'Would you believe they have run out of tonic?'

'What?' asked Akamu, his face a mask of disbelief. 'A ship this size has run out of tonic? Someone ought to be getting the sack over that. What's next? They run out of toilet paper?'

'With the size of your ass they might,' snapped Rick, getting in a quick salvo since it had been five minutes since they traded insults.

'I don't think it's the whole ship,' I got in quickly before they could wind up to full verbal battle mode. 'I think each restaurant has its own store allocated. The barman said his colleague was off trying to get more which I assume means they borrow from someone else, but he said it was there earlier.'

'Who would break into a store and steal tonic?' Rick asked.

It was a good question and another one I couldn't answer. I sipped my drink, decided it was just as rank as it looked and left it as all three of us got up to leave.

The inside of my skull was itching again. No matter what other people told me, there was something off about Dr Chouxiang and his brother and their relationship with Dr Mendoza and the lab equipment. They provided explanation for all of it, but... but... but I wasn't satisfied, basically.

When we got to the elevator, I said goodnight to Rick and Akamu, then headed back to my suite where I planned to do some digging. When I got back to my suite though, I was shocked to find someone in there waiting for me.

Ramone

I walked into my suite with a plan to pour myself the gin and tonic I couldn't get in the restaurant and spend the next hour or more on the computer being nosy. First though, my outfit for the evening was coming off. It looked good and was elegant, but I wanted to slouch around in pyjamas now.

The shoes got kicked off as I came through the door and the light jacket went on a peg in the entrance lobby. Then, as I walked into the living room, enjoying the feel of having my feet flat again, I lifted the halter neck of my dress over my head to let it hang as I started taking out my earrings.

The polite cough brought my attention across the room to where a strange man was standing.

I screamed.

He screamed because I screamed and both us of needed to find something to lean on to keep ourselves upright. I wasn't done with the screaming though, 'Get out of my cabin! Get out, get out, get out!'

The man danced about a little, trying to work out which way he was supposed to run. The main door I came in through was behind me and it was his obvious escape route but that meant having to run at me to get there. He just looked embarrassed and uncomfortable and he was doing everything he could to avoid looking at me. Under my angry gaze though, he took the only escape route he could find and went out the patio door onto the private sun terrace. Unfortunately, that doesn't lead anywhere unless one chooses to jump off the ship.

Looking sheepish once he discovered he couldn't get out that way, he came back inside but continued to stare fixedly at the floor.

I realised why; my dress was still hanging around my waist. Thankfully I had a bra on. Barbie, with her gravity defying boobs, wouldn't have worn one with such a dress, but my chest would touch my knees if I tried that. As he darted about, I turned around, pulled the neck strap back over my head and spun back to face him once more. 'Stop!' I yelled. 'Who are you?'

'I'm Ramone. The stand-in for Jermaine,' he replied, looking sheepish and embarrassed still.

'Why do I have a replacement? Oh, my life, has something happened to him? Is he okay?' Panic filled my brain as I rushed to the phone to call Dr Kim.

'I was appointed as a stand-in, madam. That's all I know, but I am certain they would have informed you if his condition had worsened.'

He was right, I knew. So, I took my thumb away from the dial button and forced myself to relax. Jermaine was strong and young and would be fine. 'I wasn't expecting a replacement,' I said for want of something to say. 'Are you moving in?'

'Only temporarily, madam. Just until Jermaine is well enough to return to duty. His cabin is set to be cleaned in the morning and I will move in after that.'

'Okay, well, I have some work to do, but I have no need for you this evening. You should retire if you wish to.'

He inclined his head in my direction. 'Very good, madam. What time should I return in the morning?'

I gave that some thought. 'I will get up around six and head to the gym. I'll be back around seven and will have breakfast at eight. So, half seven? I don't need you for anything really. I can do my own breakfast quite happily.'

Ramone smiled at me. 'I doubt the captain would approve. This is the Windsor Suite. He was most insistent that I take care of you.'

Was he really? That made me smile. Getting Jermaine, or anyone else, to do things for me went against the grain. I was a self-sufficient, blue-collar lady, but I recognised the frustration Jermaine suffered when I tried to do everything for myself, so before I sent Ramone away for the night, I threw him a bone. 'Can you mix a decent gin and tonic, Ramone?'

He was back standing on almost the exact same spot he had been when I first saw him, but at least now he was smiling. 'Madam, it is my specialty.'

Leaving him to make the drink, I went to my bedroom. I should have noticed the absent thing in my cabin, but my mind was on other things and Anna is still very new to me, so I temporarily forgot I had a dog until she exploded out of the door when I opened it.

Flying between my feet, she flew across the room at a surprising speed, barking all the while. Ramone's eyes widened as the tiny terror bore down on him. The lights in the suite were dimmed so maybe he couldn't even see what it was, but he soon found out as she went for his ankle.

'Arrgh!' he screamed like a frightened girl. 'Arrgh, what is it? Get it off, get it off.'

I didn't think Anna was actually hurting him, but she was an aggressive little monkey. Perhaps all that time spent with Japanese gangsters filled her head with violent thoughts.

Standing just a couple of feet from her as she terrorised the poor man's trouser leg, I said, 'Come, Anna,' in a very insistent voice. 'Anna, come. Anna! Anna, come!' Frustrated, I said a rude word and grabbed her. She looked out of the back of her eyes at me as if to ask why I was disturbing her when there was clearly an intruder to kill.

'Terribly sorry about that. Did she nip you?' Ramone inspected his trousers, poking a finger through a hole where she had ripped them. I pulled an apologetic face. 'She's really quite friendly,' I assured him but when he looked at her, she bared her teeth and snarled again just to prove me wrong. I took her to my bedroom with me.

Twenty minutes later, as I took a second sip of my delicious gin and tonic, I acknowledged that his boast was not unwarranted. My attention though was completely absorbed by the screen in front of my face. I had looked into Dr Mendoza and read about his career, but I was holding off on doing more because I expected Barbie to arrive any moment. I got a text from her as I was changing half an hour ago, asking if there was any update on Jermaine. She was worried about him, and well she might be, so I replied with an invite to join me. I let her know I was suspicious of the whole lab equipment story and wanted to investigate it. If nothing else, I knew it would take her mind off the concern she felt.

Reading his online profile, it was evident very quickly that Dr Mendoza was a brilliant man. He had graduated top of his class at the Cebu Institute of Medicine in the Philippines, then attended Johns Hopkins in the States where he specialised in rare disease prevention. His list of accolades was impressive with a prize from the Nobel Academy sitting at the top.

The knock at my door came just when I started reading about his family. 'Hi, Barbie.' We hugged quickly in the doorway. 'How was your day?'

'It was fairly routine all apart from the bit where Jermaine was taken away to quarantine. Do you think he will be okay?' she asked sounding worried.

I didn't know the answer to her question, but I said what people always say in such circumstances. 'I'm sure he'll pull through. He's so strong and healthy, after all.'

We reached the desk with the computer on it where a second chair was already arranged. The second chair was for me; Barbie, being thirty years younger used a computer like it was an extension of her body, where I felt like a Neanderthal bashing the keys one at a time.

'Can I get you a drink?' I asked before I settled in the chair.

'Is that gin?' she asked with a nod at my almost empty glass. 'You made it yourself?' she joked, trying to find humour in the situation.

I gave her a lopsided smile. 'Ramone made it.'

Barbie gave me a confused look. 'Ramone? Oh, little guy, shaved head?'

'That's him. He scared the bejesus out of me when I came in.' I could see that Barbie was trying to make a decision and weighing up whether she wanted to indulge or not. I helped her out. 'I'll make two.'

By the time I returned to the computer desk, Barbie was pulling up pages and trying to find the two Drs Chouxiang. 'I want to ask Dr Mendoza about his family,' I said as I sat down and handed her the drink. We clinked glasses and stared at the screen. 'Can you pull up the page I was looking at when you came in?'

A click, and there it was. Dr Mendoza's wife was also a doctor. The article we were reading didn't say how they met but she was also in disease prevention so one could assume their work brought them together. They had three children between them, all boys and the spitting image of their father.

The closeness of the family group raised a question. 'Wouldn't you bring your family if you were going on a cruise ship?' I asked.

Barbie took a sip of her drink. 'Passage time from the Philippines to Thailand is six days with the stops in between. If Dr Mendoza got on in Manila, then his round trip would be… what? Two weeks?'

'I can't guess. It would depend on what he was then doing when he arrived, but why take the ship at all? If they flew, they would arrive the same day and surely it would be cheaper too. The option to take a cruise is extravagant, but even if the money is no object; they boasted they just closed a big deal, why then not bring your family?'

Barbie pursed her lips; she didn't have an answer.

I had another question though. 'Also, if the two Dr Chouxiangs are on their way home with their fellow doctors from Thailand, of course, that's assuming they are from Thailand since that is where the ship is heading, why is Dr Mendoza with them? They are returning home and he is going with them. It feels… wrong.'

'I couldn't find them either,' said Barbie. 'The doctors, I mean. I don't know whether that is a common or rare name but I couldn't find a single Dr Chouxiang, so… that's a little suspicious.'

'It sure is. Let's keep looking.' So, we did. We didn't find them though or any of their colleagues but I only knew one name so the result wasn't conclusive. Or rather, it wasn't conclusive if I was trying to successfully argue a court case. I wasn't though and the circumstantial evidence I possessed was enough to convince me they were not who they claimed to be, and because of that, I was convinced they were up to no good.

When I said as much, Barbie asked, 'What do we do now?'

I drained my glass and sucked air in through my teeth as I made a decision. 'We find some old ladies.'

At Anchor

By the morning there was a shoreline visible from my window. The alarm woke me but now that I was awake, I wasn't so convinced I actually wanted to get out of bed. Barbie stayed until almost midnight, guiltily saying that she had to go while stifling a yawn. Looking at my clock, I knew she would be in the gym by now so it was right for her to leave when she did.

I could see the shoreline because Jermaine hadn't been here last night to draw the curtains. In the darkness at sea last night, I hadn't noticed they were open, so I awoke to sunlight coming in my window and a view for the first time since I came onboard.

The view was perplexing though. We were not due to dock in Thailand until late this afternoon and since the ship couldn't have arrived early, we had to be somewhere else. Where though?

Next to me, Anna let out a snort. She was asleep with her front paws facing one way and her back paws facing the other. One fang poked out from her top lip.

Lying in bed wasn't going to answer the question so I got up, got dressed, grabbed the dog, and got out of my suite. Despite my lethargy, I went for a run. Barbie says the only bad workout is the one you miss, so even if I half-arsed this one, it would still be better than nothing.

At six o'clock on a cruise ship you don't see many people about. Occasionally there is another person out jogging but Anna and I seemed to have the ship to ourselves as we got in our morning exercise. As the breeze tousled my hair, I ran through a few scenarios about which piece of shoreline I was looking at. When I reached the stern of the ship on my first lap, the realisation that I couldn't hear the engines brought me to a stop. The engines were off. That couldn't mean anything good.

I went right to the back of the boat and looked down into the water. Where the ocean behind the ship ought to be a maelstrom of churning waves, it was flat and calm instead. Then I went to the port side and peered over, stretching to see the anchor chain.

We were at anchor. We were at anchor in an unscheduled stop off a piece of coastline the Aurelia wasn't due to visit. This wasn't good at all. I wasted no further time staring over the side and started jogging back to my suite instead. The exercise could wait, there were questions to be answered first.

Top of the list was to do with the health of my dear friend and appointed butler, Jermaine. Ramone had not yet arrived when I got back to the suite, not that I needed him for anything, but it struck home once more that Jermaine was absent as he was always waiting for my return whenever I went out.

I called the sickbay using the ship's phone system. The woman's voice at the other end started to speak but then yawned deeply and uncontrollably. 'Sorry about that. Sickbay, Margaret speaking.'

'Good morning,' I replied, trying to put a pleasant tone into my voice as I suspected Margaret was tired because she was working too many hours right now. 'This is Patricia Fisher calling from the Windsor Suite. I was hoping you might be able to tell me if Special Rating Jermaine Clarke is recovering.'

Margaret yawned again, apologised again and consulted with someone else in the background. Then a different voice came on the line. 'Mrs Fisher, this is Dr Kim. I'm afraid his condition continues to worsen,' he said grimly. 'I wish I had better news for you. Until we are able to obtain a treatment to fight off the disease, all I can do is treat the symptoms and make the patients comfortable.'

This was the worst possible news, news I had been refusing to let myself think about. Forcing myself to focus, I asked, 'How many patients do you have now?'

Dr Kim puffed out a sigh, 'One hundred and twelve. There have been seven more reported cases in the last hour as people are waking up to discover they are sick. I expect more soon. The ship just isn't capable of handling an outbreak like this. If we don't get help soon, some of the patients…' He stopped talking suddenly, sensing he was saying what he ought not to, the fatigue from sleep-deprivation loosening his lips. 'We are anchored off West Houptiou. They have a medical facility there with an immunology department. Dr Chouxiang is liaising with them now.'

'Dr Chouxiang? He is helping you to fight this thing?'

'Of course. He and all his colleagues are chipping in and doing their best to help with patient care and diagnosis.' Dr Kim yawned again. 'Mrs Fisher, I'm sorry, I really have to go.'

I apologised for taking up so much of his time, wished him luck, and let him go. Anna nudged my foot; she wanted her breakfast. Filling her little bowl with kibble gave me something to do while I worried about Jermaine. Dr Kim made it sound like people might die from the disease. He hadn't said it, but I was certain he was about to. Could this trip end in disaster for couples and families?

Not if I could help it. There might be nothing I could do about the need for a cure, but there was something fishy going on with the team of doctors and I was going to make sure the captain knew about it.

The Captain

Alistair was clear that his job had to take priority over our blossoming relationship and had given me his mobile number on the proviso that I would not call it unless it was either an emergency or I knew him to be off duty. Given what my research had shown me last night and my failed attempt to get Commander Shriver to listen, I considered this to be the former, so I hit the dial button and waited for it to connect.

It wasn't answered though. I tried again with the same result. Okay, he was almost certainly on duty. The man worked long hours and there was something of a crisis taking place on board his ship so he was most likely on the bridge trying to deal with it. I sent a text instead.

Then I paced for ten minutes, got impatient which led to frustration and through annoyed to arrive at worried. Why wasn't Alistair taking the twenty seconds it required to answer my message? The sound of the door from Jermaine's adjoining cabin opening brought my eyes up but the bark of my attack dog got me moving.

Ramone heard her too, so just as his face appeared around the doorframe, his eyes filled with terror and vanished backwards as he slammed the door shut once more. I was going to have to buy a book on obedience training, that was for sure.

I scooped Anna into my arms yet again, stroking and calming her as I cooed in her ear to let the nice man live. 'It's okay, Ramone, I have her now. You can come in.'

'Are you sure, madam?' his muffled voice echoed back through the door.

Anna wriggled but she wasn't that difficult to keep hold of. Just to be safe though, 'I'm shutting her in my bedroom, okay? Give me thirty seconds.' With the dog safely tucked away, Ramone felt he could enter without fear for his life.

I had to wonder what she would be like if she were the size of a Labrador. The danger would be real then. I showered then dressed in jeans, pumps, and a lightweight sweater while Anna the hellhound watched me from the bed. With a swipe of mascara, I was ready to go. My handbag went over my left arm and Anna went under my right. She spared Ramone a growl as we crossed the living area to the door but once on the deck, she trotted happily along, sniffing the floor and wagging her tail.

I wanted to find someone from the crew that I knew, preferably one of the more senior members of the security team as they generally had a handle on what was happening. I could just go to the crew-only elevator that led up to the bridge, hang about there for someone to appear and grill them, but I was just as likely to be successful, and far less aggressive-looking, if I went to the upper deck restaurant. Breakfast would be on already and there were always members of the security team around. I picked Anna up again as we reached the door. It was that or she would be trying to get under tables to snag fallen bits of bacon.

Looking around, sure enough, I spotted three white uniforms that I knew as soon as I went in. Young Lieutenant Anders Pippin was getting a coffee and talking animatedly with a young couple when I approached. He shot me a smile, finished up his anecdote about a seagull and let the couple get on with their breakfast.

'Good morning, Mrs Fisher. Is there anything I can help you with?'

I went for the direct approach. 'I've been trying to make contact with the captain, I was hoping you could help me get a message to him.'

'Oh,' said Pippin.

Not picking up on his tone, I carried on, 'There is something happening on board that I believe is linked to the people getting sick. He needs to know about it right away.' I noticed Pippin was looking at the floor rather than at me. 'What is it, Anders?'

'Um, the captain is sick.'

'What!'

'Shhhh,' he insisted in a forceful but hushed tone. 'No one is allowed to know. I'm only telling you, because... well, it's you.'

'How sick is he? Does he have the virus?' I had one hand on my chest to steady my heart and all I could think was, 'Not Alistair as well.' I was so fearful for Jermaine, now I had Alistair to worry about too. Would I lose one of them? Would I lose them both? Was Barbie going to get sick next? What about Rick and Akamu? They were both much older and Dr Kim said it was having a worse effect on the very young and the very old.

Carefully, Lieutenant Pippin said, 'I don't know. I haven't seen him. All I know is the captain was taken into quarantine last night and had been sick for a while before that. Commander Shriver is now acting captain and is dealing with the emerging situation with the disease on board.'

'Did she give the order to anchor up?'

'So far as I know, yes. She is getting expert help though and is in contact with medical teams in West Houptiou. The crew have all been instructed to keep the passengers calm and monitor for anyone who looks sick. Commander Shriver expects to have drugs to combat the disease here soon.'

'She said that? I thought they hadn't identified what the disease was yet.'

'I couldn't say,' Pippin replied looking glum. 'The advice was this would be treatable and that was the message we were to give to the passengers if they ask.'

I thought about that. It sounded like a sensible message to put across. They would have to give some kind of announcement about why the ship was at anchor but admitting no one knew what the mystery illness is or how to combat it would just create panic and pandemonium. Commander Shriver was probably on top of it all and perfectly capable of managing the situation until help arrived. I needed to see Dr Kim though. I had to grill him about his helpers.

'Thank you, Anders. How are you feeling? How's your wound now?' Not very long ago the young man had been stabbed by a slightly psycho woman as he protected Barbie. Mercifully, nothing vital had been hit by the blade but he still had a very nasty cut which required surgery to fix.

With a curt nod to thank me for my concern, he said, 'It is healing, thank you. I will not be performing any sit ups for a while yet, but the doctor says I will make a full recovery.'

I thanked him for his time, excused myself and made my way to the temporary quarantine which had been created in a storeroom on deck ten. I had to check on two people I had fond feelings for, and I wouldn't be able to think straight until I knew they were still fighting. I also needed to see what the Drs Chouxiang were up to. The whole thing with them and Dr Mendoza wasn't right, but they wouldn't let me get Dr Mendoza alone to quiz him about it. That alone had my warning buzzers going crazy. Why was I the only one picking up on it though? Why wasn't Commander Shriver asking the pertinent questions?

I found out soon enough.

Sick Bay

The supposed emergency enlarged quarantine area was in a state of panic when I arrived, and it was instantly obvious why: it was full, and more people were arriving. There was a reception desk set up in the passageway outside the doors and a queue of people trying to get in. Not all of them were sick, of course, some of the people queuing were bringing their loved ones for treatment, no doubt directed here by members of the crew.

Quarantine restrictions looked to be out the window too; Dr Kim and the rest of the medical staff were simply overrun. As two orderlies shoved their way through the crowd with a patient on a stretcher, I followed them in uninvited, holding on to his arm as if I was the sick man's relative.

Inside, I paused and scanned around for Alistair but I needed to find Dr Kim before I did anything else. Anna wriggled under my arm, licking my chin when I cooed at her. I spotted the exhausted Dr Kim on the far side of the room, consulting a chart at the foot of someone's bed. He had his back to me so didn't see me approach.

'Dr Kim,' I called as I weaved between the lines of beds. He turned to see who had spoken and I saw his face for the first time since yesterday. 'Dr Kim, how long has it been since you slept?'

He shrugged. 'A while.' Then he gave me a half-hearted smile. 'It reminds me of my junior doctor years actually. It's kind of fun to be this tired again. Some of my colleagues poked fun at me when I took this job, saying it was a retirement home for failed doctors who wanted to get a good suntan. I guess the joke's on me.'

'Are you having any luck in treating them?' I asked.

He hung his head and shook it. 'None at all. The presentation is like a fast-acting version of haemorrhagic fever, what people more commonly refer to as Ebola. Treatment for that should be give intravenous fluids, oxygen and then treat the symptoms to reduce fluids lost through vomiting and diarrhoea. We just don't have the supplies to treat this many people so only the sickest are getting anything.'

'I was told Commander Shriver has a plan to obtain a cure from West Houptiou.'

Dr Kim gave me an uncertain look. 'I don't see how that's possible. I know Dr Chouxiang made contact with a disease control centre on the mainland. That's why we are at anchor. They wouldn't let us dock, quite rightly, of course, but have offered to send a team aboard to assist with treatment.'

'What does Dr Mendoza think? He's the world leader on tackling rare infectious diseases, isn't he?'

Wearily, Dr Kim nodded. 'Dr Mendoza isn't acting normally. Not that I know the man, not really anyway. He is taking his inability to treat the patients personally and he has a strange relationship with Dr Chouxiang. The elder Dr Chouxiang that is. The two are inseparable, though I get the impression Dr Mendoza would rather work alone.' Dr Kim shrugged again. 'I don't know. I might be imagining the whole thing. There they are now though, working on the same patient.'

Dr Kim flicked his head toward the two men. They were across the wide expanse of the open makeshift ward and out of earshot. I was about to change that though. 'Thank you, Dr Kim. Can you please tell me where the captain is?'

'I'll take you to him.' As we walked, Dr Kim explained that he tried to put the captain in a private room, but Alistair had argued and insisted he get no different treatment to everyone else suffering. If anything, he wasn't to have a bed at all if it meant someone else went without. That certainly sounded like something Alistair would say.

'How is he now?' I asked. Without answering my question, Dr Kim had led me across the room, weaving between beds. I looked ahead in the direction we were going expecting to see the face I recognised or hear his voice. When Dr Kim stopped at a bed, I had to look twice to see that the gaunt, pale face poking above the sheets was indeed Alistair Huntley.

'He lost consciousness about an hour ago. He must have been fighting it for some time before he revealed he was sick.'

I put my hand to my mouth. Honestly, if Dr Kim had told me he was dead I would have believed him. Only the faint but steady rise and fall of his chest gave away that he was still alive. 'Oh, my life,' I murmured. 'How bad is it?'

'I can't talk about that, Mrs Fisher. Suffice to say we need help in the form of medical staff and supplies right now and we will not be able to revive some of the sick without proper medical treatment.' He gripped my arm. 'You should go, Mrs Fisher. I am already beginning to feel the effects. The longer you expose yourself, the more likely it is that you will get sick.'

With those chill words ringing in my ears, and with a sorrowful pat on Alistair's arm, I took myself away. I didn't go far though, Dr Mendoza and Dr Chouxiang were just a few beds over, and they were arguing.

'I said I'm not leaving,' insisted Dr Mendoza. 'I am responsible for the condition of these people. I cannot just let them suffer like this.'

'Why are you responsible?' I asked, approaching from behind both men so they spun around to see who had spoken.

'Ah, Mrs Fisher,' said Dr Chouxiang. 'Again,' he added to make a point. 'What can we do for you?'

'Dr Mendoza just said the patients' ill-health was his responsibility. What do you mean by that Dr Mendoza?'

Dr Mendoza looked nervous when he started talking, cutting his eyes at his colleague to see what he was doing. 'I, ah.'

Dr Chouxiang spoke over the top of him. 'What Dr Mendoza means is that he is the world leader on diseases of this type and were he further along with his research, he might already have a treatment available. Isn't that right, Dr Mendoza.'

Staring at the floor guiltily, Dr Mendoza nodded. 'Yes, that's right. That's what I was trying to say.'

To bring his eyes up to meet mine, I tapped Dr Mendoza on his hand. 'I wonder if I might have a moment of your time in private.'

Dr Mendoza shot a panicked look at his colleague. Dr Chouxiang just crossed his arm and gave me a curious look. 'Dr Mendoza has patients to attend to, Mrs Fisher. Your needs cannot take priority over them. Since you are clearly not sick and are only detracting from our efforts with your senseless enquiries, I suggest you escape this place while you can.' He was very clear about his desire to keep me away from Dr Mendoza though I still didn't know why.

However, when I glanced at Dr Mendoza the next second, the nervous looking man cast his eyes down in a deliberate gesture. 'Mrs Fisher,' prompted Dr Chouxiang, 'it is time to go.'

I looked back at Dr Mendoza and he did the thing with his eyes again. I glanced down and could see that he was trying to trace a word into the dust on the floor with the toe of his shoe. I tried to stare at it but didn't want Dr Chouxiang to follow my gaze and see that Dr Mendoza was trying to pass me a message in secret.

The opportunity was lost though when Dr Chouxiang stepped forward to usher me away and stepped onto whatever it was Dr Mendoza wanted me to see. 'Enough now, Mrs Fisher. It is not safe for you here. That alone should convince you to leave.'

As he came close, Anna took offense at his proximity and lunged forward to snap at him. I almost dropped her, but the bark brought the attention of a nearby nurse who added her insistence that I leave.

Unable to argue, I let her usher me from the awful sick bay. Back outside in the passageway, I plopped Anna back on the floor and chewed my lip. I had a lot of things to do and the length of time in which I had to get them done was to be determined by how long the weakest patients had left – a period I couldn't possibly determine.

Was I even right about Dr Chouxiang though? Only time would tell. Giving Anna's lead a quick tug to get her moving in the right direction, I set off to gather a team.

Pick Pockets

'Tell me where we are going again,' demanded Rick as both he and Akamu shuffled after me. 'My bunions are giving me hell, dammit.'

'Stop complaining, you old woman,' snapped Akamu. If there was one thing for certain, no matter what I asked Rick and Akamu to do, they were going to whine and moan and battle each other and do a great job anyway.

'We are heading back to General Tso's restaurant,' I said over my shoulder as I led them to the elevators. It had taken me a while to find them because they were not in their cabin when I went to it. Contrary to my expectations, no announcement had been made to tell the passengers why the Aurelia was now at anchor two miles off the coast. Commander Shriver must have something planned but despite the worry I sensed among some groups, nervous chatter giving a sense of unrest, in general, people were getting on and enjoying themselves. Rick and Akamu had followed the crowd and when I found them, they were on the eighteenth deck lido relaxing on sun beds. Akamu had been asleep, snoring loudly with his hat over his face. When I approached, Rick had been slowly attempting to lower Akamu's right hand into a bowl of water, a frat boy trick his friend would not thank him for.

Now they were following me because I had a task for them and couldn't get everything done by myself.

Squinting at his watch because he didn't have his reading glasses on, Rick said, 'Surely the restaurant isn't open this early. It's... it's only just after ten o'clock, Patricia.'

'That's what I'm counting on.' I didn't expand on that statement and the guys were generous and trusting enough to continue shuffling after me. Unlike a business in a town, the restaurant had no front door to it. The ornate entrance, with a dragon adorning each side had a sign saying closed to deter passengers from going in, but there was no physical barrier preventing our entry.

Inside, there were cleaners polishing glass and buffing those bits deemed worthy of buffing and the person I wanted to see; a barman behind the bar. 'Good morning,' I said breezily on my direct path to him.

His head came up. 'Sorry, we're closed. Dinner reservations can be made using the onboard system or via your app or you can come by later when one of the servers are here. I'm just in to restock the bar.'

'Yes, thank you. It's you that I came to see.' The man's eyebrows took off to the top of his head where they tried to touch his hairline. He wasn't one of the men that had been working last night and he was dressed differently, wearing a standard crew uniform not the ornate Chinese brocaded outfit the staff that worked here wore.

'How can I help?' he asked, putting his tablet to one side.

I pointed to the tablet as Rick and Akamu caught up to me and fanned out on either side. 'Are you doing a stocktake?' The man looked at the tablet, then back at me, questions about why I wanted to know forming a queue in his head. 'I ask because last night they ran out of tonic water here.'

'Yeah, they couldn't make her a gin and tonic,' laughed Rick. 'I thought the world was going to end.'

His comment put the barman on the defensive. 'If you wish to complain, I'm not the one to complain to. Someone stole the tonic, that's all I know. I got hell about it from my manager this morning because he thinks I must have failed to count it properly. Accused me of skipping the physical checks and guessing the numbers so I could skive off.'

I help up my hands to calm him. 'No complaints. But what if you could show your manager that the tonic was stolen and then present him with the culprits?' He eyed me to see if I was messing him about. He was hooked. 'I think I know who is behind this and I need you to help these two gentlemen with their investigation.'

'Investigation?' all three men said at once.

'Yes.' Still looking at the barman, I said, 'I'm Patricia Fisher. What's your name?'

Unlike most crew, he wasn't wearing a name badge. He was moving his lips though. 'Patricia Fisher. Patricia Fisher. Where do I know that name from?'

'She's the one that found the giant sapphire and had a shootout with a load of gangsters in the cabaret theatre,' provided Akamu with a chuckle.

'Yeah, that's it!' said the barman. 'I'm John.'

'Well, John, these two gentleman are retired police officers and would like to help you track down the missing tonic. It shouldn't take too long.' I turned around to speak to my two friends. 'I have a good idea what is going on here, but I have matters elsewhere to attend to. Can I leave this with you?'

'Sure,' said Rick.

'No problem,' echoed Akamu. 'You know they do have an onboard security team that is really good at handling issues such as this.'

'Yes, but what fun would that be? Give me a call when you find them?'

'Find who?' Rick called after me, but I was already on my way out the door.

Telegram

Sitting in the corner of the gym, I waited patiently for Barbie to finish her class rather than interrupt. She was happily destroying a dozen fit looking men; funny how almost all the blonde bombshell's classes were filled with men. They had weights above their heads as she had them squat and press and twist and bend to a thumping bass beat. All the while she was shouting encouragement and commands and barely even sweating while the men in her class looked like they had been out in the rain for an hour. Most of them were standing in a pool of their own perspiration.

I needed her help. Or rather, I needed the help of someone who was good with computers. I could have asked one of the ship's security team, and honestly, Baker or Bhukari or one of the other lieutenants I had got to know well might have been a more appropriate choice given the nature of my investigations, but I knew where to find Barbie and I knew I could rely on her.

As the class ended, I stood up. Anna had been balanced on my lap but was back under my right arm as I made my way around the sweaty men to get to my friend. 'I need your expertise, come on,' I said as I grabbed her arm. 'No time to lose.'

'Hold on I need my towel,' she said as I pulled her along.

'You look perfect. I have a towel you can use in my suite.' I really didn't feel like we could waste any more time.

'Right. Impatient much? Where are we going?' In the short walk to my suite I explained about Dr Mendoza's panicked eyes and the message he was trying to give me. Barbie said, 'You know, from anyone else, this would sound like lunacy. Since it's you, I guess we have to look into it.'

Thankful that she was onboard, I pushed my way into my suite, dropped my handbag on a couch as I crossed the room and let Anna go once I was sure Ramone wasn't lurking in the kitchen.

Barbie hit the power button on the computer and went to get water from the fridge. 'Stay hydrated,' she advised as she handed me a bottle too. 'Brain works better when it is hydrated.' Back at the desk she asked, 'So what are we looking for?'

'I want to track down his family. Dr Mendoza isn't acting like a normal person would act. To start with he claimed that the people getting sick was his fault.'

'What did he mean by that?'

'I'm not sure, but Dr Chouxiang was very quick to cover it up. He looks nervous all the time, Dr Mendoza that is. Like he can't say what he wants to say and is being monitored the whole time. I got the sense that they are holding something over him, and he was trying to give me a clue about what it might be.'

'So, you want to track down his family,' Barbie confirmed. 'I should be able to find an address easily enough but it will take a while. If you want to talk to them, I'll need to find a phone number and that might be a bit trickier. What do you want to ask them?'

I drummed my fingers on the table as I considered her question. I was proposing to track down a man's family in Manilla and ask them… what? Has your husband been kidnapped? That was the impression I got but for that to be true, there then had to be a compelling reason for him to stay with them when it would be easy enough for him to alert the ship's security and get their protection. 'I need to check if they are alive.'

'Um, what?' said Barbie, staring at me now instead of the screen.

'I hope I'm wrong, but I think Dr Mendoza might be here because his family is being held captive. That feels right; it links the pieces as I see them.'

Barbie spun the swivel chair around to face me, sensing that I was onto something but needed to talk it through. 'Ok. Let's say you're right. To what end are they holding his family captive? What do they gain from it?'

'They want him to do something,' I blurted. 'He's the world's leading immunologist and we have a rare disease loose on board this ship. Are they trying to target someone on this ship and kill them?' My eyes widened as I saw the possibilities stretching out. 'Stop the search for his family. Look at dignitaries onboard instead. Politicians, powerful businessmen, anyone linked with West Houptiou.'

Barbie's fingers were flying over the keyboard. 'Why West Houptiou?'

'Because that's where we have miraculously found ourselves anchored.' Barbie nodded her understanding, but I got up to pace as she continued to pull together information. There was something I was missing here. Something vital that linked the parts somehow.

A knock at the door disturbed my train of thought. Instantly awake, Anna flew off the couch she had been curled up asleep on and threw herself at the door. Then Ramone entered the suite from the door in the kitchen and the little dog switched flank to attack the visible target instead.

Ramone's eyes went wide but this time he was ready for her. He crouched down in the kitchen as the barking menace charged him then stood up triumphantly with the dog held between two oven gloves. He still needed to answer the door, so on his way through the cabin, he handed over my tiny, angry but also now confused dog.

Whoever was outside knocked again, eliciting a further round of bonkers barking from Anna who was now wriggling in my grip to be set free. At much the same glacial pace that Jermaine would take when moving around the apartment, Ramone arrived finally at the main entrance to my suite and answered the door.

He exchanged a few words and was handed something fancy on a silver tray. It looked like an envelope. Not an ordinary envelope though I saw as he closed the door and came my way; the envelope shone like it was imbued with sunlight.

'You have a telegram, madam,' Ramone announced as he held the tray out for me, his right hand extended, his left hand behind his back.

'A telegram?' said Barbie, getting up to see what I had. 'What's a telegram?

'It like a text message from a century ago except it took days to get to its recipient,' I mumbled as I stared at the envelope.

'Is that gold?' Barbie asked sounding a little awestruck.

The envelope was indeed embossed with gold leaf which made me curious because a telegram was a transcribed message sent along a fixed wire between two devices. Or at least that was how I thought of it. I was thirty years older than Barbie, but telegrams had gone the way of the dodo long before I was born. This though had to have come through the post which was then even more odd because we were at sea and the postman couldn't get to us.

'How did this get here?' I asked, the question clearly aimed at Ramone.

'The courier arrived by helicopter to hand deliver it, madam.' A helicopter to deliver an envelope? Now this was strange.

Poor Ramone was still standing with one arm extended and the heavy silver tray balanced on it. I handed Anna to Barbie and took the telegram from the tray to hold it in front of me for closer inspection. I could feel the sunlight coming through my windows and reflecting off the gold to light up my face.

'Who is it from, Patty? Come on, open it!' Barbie demanded.

I turned it over to find it was sealed. Ramone coughed politely and reached up to unfold a piece of cloth on the tray which revealed a silver letter opener. I slit along the top of the envelope, genuinely feeling bad that I had ruined its perfection, then drew out the contents to read. It was a single piece of paper, but it had the same gold embossed pattern running down both sides and looked to be about the finest paper I had ever held.

Dear Mrs Fisher

I trust this note will find you in good health and enjoying your cruise. You recently performed a most blessed service for both me and my country when you returned the sapphire to us. The jewel was believed forever lost and my father, who blamed himself for allowing it to be displayed, died peacefully and contentedly two days after its return. I believe your gift to us allowed him to enter the next realm satisfied that his life here was complete.

As a token of gratitude for this service, I wish to invite you and your friends to join me at my coronation in Zangrabar. If you are willing, it is my intent to collect you from the dock in Mumbai when the ship is due to sail. You will be flown on my personal jet and treated as a visiting royal family. You may stay as my guests for as long as you wish or you can be returned to the Aurelia when it docks at its next port.

During your all-expenses-paid stay, I may ask a small favour of you; I have a mystery I hope you may solve.

My courier will return your answer.

I remain your servant,

Dundegan Zebradim

Maharaja of Zangrabar

As my eyes got to the end and went back to start reading it again, Barbie said, 'Wow.' It wasn't an exclamation though, more a reverent exhaling of stunned disbelief. 'That's a letter from an actual Maharaja. Isn't he, like, the third richest man on the planet?'

'Something like that,' I murmured as my eyes skipped over the letter again. A personal note of thanks from the Maharaja, an invitation to attend his coronation and a request for my help. I backed into my chair and sat down. 'Ooh, I feel a little light headed.'

Barbie sat next to me. 'Will you go?'

'I shall need to give that some thought,' I replied, still stunned by the invitation to a royal event. Then I remembered the open invitation to bring friends, the unlimited nature of the invite undoubtedly deliberate. 'What do you think? Do you want to go?'

'Me?'

'Well who else would I take? If I go, I'm not going by myself and you and Jermaine are top of the list, not least because the sapphire would never have been recovered without your help.'

'A Maharaja's coronation,' she said dreamily. 'That sounds ever so grand.'

'It sounds like a once in a lifetime opportunity,' I added. 'We have to go, don't we?'

'What about the mystery he wants you to solve for him? He didn't say what it was. Maybe it's dangerous.'

'It can't be more dangerous than staying onboard this ship.' My offhand comment brought me back to ground with a bump. 'We need to get on with solving the mystery here first.'

Ramone was waiting expectantly with his silver tray though and the courier was still standing just inside the door. 'Please tell the Maharaja I will be waiting in Mumbai as requested. I look forward to meeting him.'

I got a quiet, 'Yay!' from Barbie.

The courier inclined his head and left, Ramone closing the door behind him and I turned my attention back to the computer. The decision was made; Barbie, Jermaine, and I were going to Zangrabar.

All I had to do now was save Jermaine's life.

Tricky Phone Calls

I stared into nothing, worrying about Jermaine and Alistair and everyone else as Barbie and I each ate a bowl of rainbow couscous. Filled with all manner of earthy, healthy grains and pulses and bits of seed, it was like eating kitty litter, but I knew it was good for me, so I stuck with it.

The lunch was taken to give our eyes and brains a break. After more than two hours of digging, Barbie and I had eliminated the idea that they might be targeting a person of interest on board. There were thousands of guests but not one from West Houptiou and very few persons we could find who had any connection to government service. There were rich people on the Aurelia, of course there were, but finding a connection between them and Dr Chouxiang or less specifically, West Houptiou, was too difficult so we dismissed it.

Having done so, we focused our attention back on finding a home address for the Mendoza family. Barbie managed to piece together enough information from different articles to get a general sense of where they were, then used the Manilla phone book to eliminate some of the Mendoza options listed, scrubbing addresses in retirement homes or in poor areas. With six options left on her list, we started calling them.

Call it luck, call it geography, whatever it is, the only language I speak is English and that is what they speak in the Philippines too. They speak Filipino too, so it's an entire nation of polyglots, but their English ability meant I could just call them and wouldn't need a translator.

In front of me I had a note pad filled with details of Dr Mendoza's family; names and ages and suchlike. It was information we had needed to find but which I now planned to use to determine if the person I was speaking to was who they said they were. This was assuming I even found the right house, of course.

The first call wasn't answered and the second was not the family of a doctor. On the third attempt, I struck gold.

'Hello.' The voice was male and sounded unhappy to be answering the phone. It was also accented and to my ear sounded just like Dr Chouxiang.

'Good afternoon, this is Sylvia Stokes, I'm the legal council for John Hopkins Hospital here in the States.' I got a thumbs up from Barbie. 'I need to speak with Dr Bayani Mendoza. Can you please confirm I have the right number for him?'

'This is the right number, but he is away on business currently. He will not be back for some time.'

'Would it be possible to speak to his wife instead, please?' I kept my tone professionally polite to allay any suspicion. My senses were already firing though. Who was the unnamed man in the Mendoza household?

'One moment,' he said, and the line went quiet.

A few seconds later, a new voice came on the line. This time it was a woman's voice and did not carry the same accent. 'This is Carmela Mendoza. How can I help you?' I repeated my introduction. She was quiet at the other end when I finished. When she finally spoke, she said, 'I don't remember a Sylvia Stokes. I was in John Hopkins last week.'

This was better. I was talking to his wife, so now I could ask a direct question about her husband. But as I opened my mouth, a voice of caution made me tread carefully. I glanced down at the list of names and family details on my desk and pitched a curve ball. 'Oh, well, we met, actually. You told me all about your son, little Danni. I'm the tall red head who wore a pinstripe suit and spilled coffee all down my white blouse. You must remember that.'

There was a pause when I thought she was going to call me out, then she laughed. 'Yes, of course. How could I forget. What can I do for you?'

I felt the blood drain from my face; I was right. There was a woman pretending to be Dr Mendoza's wife. She didn't even know the names of her children so there was no ambiguity in my mind. I played along for another minute, saying that it was really her husband I needed to speak to. I still had no idea what was going on, but I didn't want them to sense we were on to them. When I found a natural break in the conversation, I said goodbye and hung up.

'Do you think they are ok?' asked Barbie. 'His family, I mean.'

She was asking me if they were already dead, a question to which I didn't have an answer, but I chose to assume they were alive and unharmed and could yet be rescued. 'We don't know. I think they will keep them alive though because Dr Mendoza may demand proof of life from his captors.'

'Proof of life?'

'Yes. When people are taken hostage, the negotiators often ask for proof of life. They want to speak with the hostage or hostages to prove to themselves they are still alive. I think Dr Mendoza has been tricked into infecting the people on this ship and the team led by Dr Chouxiang are all behind it.'

'Oh, my,' gasped Barbie. 'Why would they do that?'

I shook my head. 'I don't know yet. But I intend to find out. We need help though. We have to get this to Commander Shriver. As acting captain, she can bring down the full might of the ship's security team on them.'

Would she though?

Hatching a Plot

My relationship with Commander Shriver was tenuous on a good day. After the incident yesterday and the added pressure she must be feeling, I doubted today counted as a good day. That was why Barbie made the phone call to the bridge. Like all crew she had access codes to use parts of the ship's phone system set aside for crew use. She wasn't happy about it though, referring to the senior officer as prickly.

I stood by and listened as she was put through to the bridge. 'Hello. Yes, this is Special Rating Berkeley, I need to speak with Commander Shriver or whoever she has appointed as the new deputy captain, please.' There was a pause while she listened. 'She hasn't appointed a new deputy captain? How can that work?' Another pause. 'She says she doesn't need one?' I listened with increasing worry knitting my brow. 'Will it be possible to speak with her? I have pertinent information she really needs to hear.'

This time the pause was longer and it was clear the person at the other end had walked away from the phone. Barbie and I locked eyes, the worry in her eyes reflected in mine. The calm, steady hand of Captain Alistair Huntley was no longer guiding the ship and Acting Captain Shriver was not doing well in his place. Was it just bedding-in nerves? Just because someone said she had refused to appoint a new deputy captain, didn't mean it was true. It could just be that she found other tasks which had to take priority?

The wait stretched out several minutes so that when a voice finally echoed in Barbie's ear, her thoughts had wandered off and the sound made her jump. She dropped the phone, juggled it, caught it, and managed to get it back to her ear.

'Right. Thank you.' She placed the phone gently back in its cradle. Then tipped her head back and screamed in frustration. The noise woke Anna, once again asleep on the couch. 'She is too busy to see me or even come to the phone to speak to me.'

'Then we'll have to go to her. This is too big for us to let it go and too big for her to ignore once she understands what we are talking about.' I was giving her the benefit of the doubt. 'Look at this from her perspective. She was only appointed as deputy captain two weeks ago, a role she came to after the previous two incumbents lasted a grand total of only two weeks and the man before that went to jail. She is facing the biggest crisis this ship, or perhaps even this shipping line, or perhaps even any cruise ship in history has faced since the Titanic hit an iceberg and her mentor is incapacitated. She is acting like this because she doesn't have the facts that we have. Once we explain what we know, she will come around.'

Barbie frowned. 'I sure hope you're right, Patty.'

Grimly, I set my jaw and said, 'Let's go find out.' Then turned to Anna, who glanced at me, decided I looked like I was about to make her do something and pretended to be asleep. She would be nothing but trouble on this outing, so I escorted her to my bedroom where she could sleep on the bed until my return.

Since we couldn't talk to Commander Shriver via the ship's phone system, the remaining choice was to visit the bridge in person. A trickier proposition because passengers were not allowed up there except by invitation and the elevator to get there was security coded and often guarded. Barbie, who was a member of crew, was not in a role where access to the bridge was something she would ever need, so she didn't know the access codes to use the elevator even if it wasn't guarded.

It wasn't a long walk to get there, but my sense of dread over getting to see Commander Shriver grew with each step. As it was, I got a reprieve when Rick called.

I fished around in my bag to find my phone, its incessant ringing finally shutting off as I picked it up. 'Hi, Rick, what've you got?'

He chuckled at me. 'I don't know how you do it, Patricia. Your nose is something else; you're like a bloodhound. We haven't gone in yet, but we can see them.'

'Okay, I'm on my way.' I put the phone away and changed direction. 'We have another task to perform first. We need to find a couple of friendly security team though.'

I didn't explain further and hadn't warned Barbie of my intention to delay the visit to the bridge so she carried on several yards before she realised I was no longer with her and had to run to catch up again.

'Where are we going now?' she asked, confused about the change in tactic.

Without breaking stride, I did my best to explain, 'You remember I told you about the supply of tonic going missing?'

'Yeah.'

'I had Rick and Akamu working on it while we were looking into Dr Mendoza's family. They have the culprits cornered now.'

'Don't we just need ship security to take them into custody? Why are we going?'

'Because I think we need to enlist their help.' I left it at that, my final comment deliberately cryptic.

'Patty, you are so mysterious,' Barbie giggled as she danced ahead to press the elevator call button.

As she watched the light on the panel above the door to show her which deck the car was on, I said, 'Hold on. We still need to find Baker or Schneider or Pippin or anyone we know from the security team. I usually go to the upper deck restaurant because they go in there for coffee.'

Barbie reached around to her left hip where she kept her phone in a little pouch in her form-fitting leggings. 'I can just call them. Deepa and I are good friends. I have her number.' Wondering why I hadn't thought of that earlier, I leaned against the wall next to the elevator and thought about what I would need to say to Acting Captain Shriver.

Listening to half a conversation again, it sounded like Barbie got through but was then struggling to make out what was being said. I watched her place her spare hand over her ear and screw up her face as if that would help her hear. After a few seconds she gave up. 'She's somewhere with a poor signal.'

Then the elevator pinged, and Lieutenant Deepa Bhukari stepped out with Lieutenant Baker. Two of my favourite crew delivered right to me. Deepa and Barbie laughed at the irony of their conversation because Barbie had been saying she was waiting by the elevator and Deepa was saying she couldn't hear because she was in an elevator.

I guided them back in and explained what we were doing. Twelve floors down, the doors opened to reveal John the barman. I guess the guys sent him because he moved a lot faster than they did.

'Oh good,' John the barman said. 'You brought security with you. Not sure you'll need it with these two though,' he chuckled.

Baker huffed, 'Don't bet on it. These two are slippery.'

'What two?' asked Barbie. 'Who are we are here for?'

John the barman led the way, 'You'll see.' While Barbie frowned at being the only one that didn't know what was going on, John led us along a passageway and around a corner and along another passageway and as we turned yet another corner, Rick and Akamu came into sight. They had their backs to us and were peering through a door.

As we neared them, John dropped his voice to a whisper. 'This is the storeroom we found them in. It was a bit like following the mess a mouse makes to find the mouse.'

Rick and Akamu heard us and ducked away from the door. 'They led us quite the merry dance. We found them more by a process of elimination in the end. They had been taking provisions from almost every store but when we couldn't find them in any of those, we started looking in the ones that hadn't been stolen from.'

'How were they getting in and out?' asked Deepa. 'The lock looks intact.'

It was Akamu that replied. 'They've been picking them. These dames have some skills, I tell you. They pick each lock to get in, then shut the locks again afterwards. We might never have caught them if Patricia hadn't said to check where there was a cold store.'

'It was obvious.'

'What was?' asked Barbie. 'Seriously, if someone doesn't tell me what is going on, I will get really, really snippy soon.'

It wasn't the best threat I had received recently but for Barbie it was strong stuff. 'Inside this storeroom somewhere are Agnes Eldritch and Mavis Du Maurier. They are a pair of professional thieves. I met them a few days ago in the upper deck restaurant. I thought they were there to have dinner, but in retrospect they were probably eyeing up people to rob. We busted them picking pockets with another couple.'

'We don't know that for certain,' Baker interrupted.

'No, we don't,' I conceded. 'I think we can get them to confess though. Anyway,' I picked up the story again, 'they ordered gin at the exact same time as me and the two barmen reached for the same bottle of Hendricks. We laughed about it, but I knew they were gin drinkers and were at large somewhere on the ship. So, when I heard the tonic was going missing, I added up the clues and had these two miscreants track them down.'

Rick nudged Akamu. 'She's talking about you there, jackass.'

'Well done, Mrs Fisher,' said Lieutenant Bhukari with a nod of appreciation. 'I feel it's about time we got them, don't you?'

Rick raised a hand. 'There's more than one door to this place. We need to split up and enter from both sides at the same time.' A quick plan was hatched, and we split up. Rick, Deepa, and I staying where we were, Akamu, Barbie, and Baker making their way to the other door. The two security officers switched their radios to another channel so they could talk to each other and not be heard by everyone else, then counted down to zero and we all walked calmly into the store.

Agnes and Mavis

Sneaking into the storeroom we got a good look at the two old ladies. They had made a little makeshift house using a pair of polypropylene chairs they had found somewhere and some boxes they had thrown an old cloth over. It looked like they were sitting around a table with a tablecloth on it. All that was missing was a vase of flowers in the middle. Each had an empty glass in front of them and several discarded food wrappers where they had survived on snacks in their little hideaway.

The caterwauling started the second they saw us. 'I told you we would get caught, you daft old bat,' said one, swiping at the other with her paperback book.

'It's because you couldn't manage without a cold store for your tonic. That's why we got caught, Mavis.'

'No, it isn't,' Mavis argued. 'Besides, we both want the tonic cold. It's bad enough that we don't have ice, how are we supposed to drink it warm?'

Neither one of the ladies had yet paid the six people in front of them any attention at all. When Lieutenant Baker cleared his throat, Agnes waved a hand in his direction but didn't turn her head. 'We'll get to you in a minute, deary. Now, where was I? Oh, yes. Take that, Mavis Du Maurier.' Then she launched her paperback book at the other woman's head.

It bounced off but before it could reach the floor Mavis had hold of her walking stick and was swinging it at her accomplice with an apparent intent to do harm.

Baker stepped forward and caught it mid-swing. 'That's quite enough of that, thank you, ladies.'

John the barman poked his head in the cold store they were sitting next to. 'I found the tonic. How much of it did you steal?'

'All of it,' boasted Mavis. 'If you're going to pull a heist, make it a big one, eh?'

'You don't know when to shut up, do you Mavis?' complained her partner. 'That silly nonsense about always going big was what got us caught in Dublin.'

'That was thirty-seven years ago, Agnes. Are you never going to let that go?' They took to bickering even as Lieutenant Baker moved in to help Mavis get to her feet. They both looked wobbly and frail and I wondered if we might have to arrange for wheelchairs or something to get them around the ship. It was a long walk back to the elevators, after all.

Mavis accepted Lieutenant Baker's hand and made a show of trying to get up, so he put a bit more effort into it to pull her onto her feet. That's when she showed us just how wily she was. As he threw his bodyweight backwards, she went with him, leaping to her feet and shoving him away.

As if reacting to a silent cue, Agnes was also on her feet, lunging forward with her own walking stick to whack Baker hard between his legs. As he sucked in a sharp breath, both Rick and Akamu winced but there was no time to deal with Baker's injury, the old ladies were making a break for it.

They had lulled us into a false sense of security with their old lady act but were sprightly and capable and arguably dangerous.

Lieutenant Bhukari tasered them both.

As they lay on the floor twitching and making rude gestures at us with their jerky hands, Rick nudged Akamu. 'I like them.'

Half an hour later, we had them in an interview room where they were to be questioned. Barbie took herself back to the gym as she had another class to teach, but Rick, Akamu and I were too entertained to go anywhere.

Agnes and Mavis were not cooperative, so Lieutenant Baker called for backup before he attempted to move them. Even then, they kept trying to escape as they were led from the storeroom to the interview room we were now in and were now sullenly silent in the two chairs opposite Baker and me.

Baker was asking the questions. 'I'm curious, ladies. How were you planning to get off the ship once we docked in Phuket? That was our next intended port, but ship security would be looking out for you.'

'Hah!' scoffed Agnes. 'Ship security couldn't catch us if they tried.'

'They did catch us,' Mavis pointed out. Waving her arm around to indicate their surroundings. 'We are, one might say, caught.'

'Yes, but if they hadn't caught us, they would never have been able to catch us,' Agnes claimed triumphantly. We all took a moment to think about that one.

Mavis spoke up. 'Yes, well, we would have disguised ourselves and slipped off as crew probably. This isn't our first radio.'

'Rodeo,' corrected Agnes with a sad shake of her head.

'Huh?'

'Rodeo. This isn't out first rodeo.' Agnes tutted. 'You always get it wrong and you make us sound like dummies.'

Rick had a question. 'How many radios, um, I mean rodeos are we talking about exactly?' They both looked at him. 'I mean, how long have you been stealing things on board cruise ships?'

The two women exchanged a glance. 'Not long,' said Agnes slowly, looking at her partner for confirmation. 'A decade maybe.'

'A decade,' echoed Bhukari, sounding stunned.

'Yeah, we came to it quite late in our careers,' added Mavis. 'We were getting a bit old for jewellery stores and burgling penthouse suites.'

'Goodness, yeah, it was much easier to rob playboys when we were younger and could just seduce them. It was a different city every week then. Offer a man a night with two pretty girls and he would have us in his penthouse suite before you could blink. Then we would get him naked, tie him up, empty his safe and walk out.'

'They never reported it,' bragged Mavis. 'Too embarrassed I guess but as we got older the rejections got more frequent so by the time we were in our forties we had to switch tactics.'

'Yeah, it's not easy being an honest career thief once you're middle-aged,' added Agnes. It was fascinating to hear the two women talk and they seemed only too happy to open up about it all. Like they were excited to finally have an audience, they bragged about their achievements and rattled off hundreds upon hundreds of crimes committed over more than five decades.

They were younger than I thought too. They wore makeup to disguise themselves as octogenarians, carrying walking sticks and exaggerating their aching knees but were both sixty-eight and met at school when they both broke into the school tuck shop to rob it. They moved on from stealing candy as school children to bigger crimes and as adults, travelling around the world with stolen cash and jewels, staying in fine hotels so they could rob the clientele and always getting out of the country before anyone could find them.

'The world is a big place,' Agnes commented sagely at one point.

Though they were entertaining, they were also exactly what they said: career criminals and as such the only thing Baker and Bhukari could do was lock them up and hand them over to the authorities at some point. Who got them was a problem I didn't want to sort out; they were most likely wanted in half the countries on the planet and their latest crime spree had taken place in international waters.

Baker rapped his knuckles on the table. 'I think that will about do it for this afternoon's story session. Fascinating though it was, I'm afraid the time has come for me to escort these ladies to the brig.'

For the last few hours I had been toying with a slightly crazy plan. Crazy even for me, I mean. Now I had to either get on with it or forget it, but when an image of Alistair's sick face swam into my consciousness, I grabbed Baker's arm.

'We can't,' I said. 'We need them.'

'We need them?' said every single person in the room.

All eyes were on me with a look of confusion on every face, except for Agnes and Mavis who just looked hopeful. I slouched back into my chair and breathed out deeply. I needed to get it all straight in my head and I was finding it difficult to work out all the moving parts.

Then, before the room's occupants could get impatient with me, I started to outline what I believed, what I suspected, what I wanted to do and told them what would happen if we didn't do it.

When I finished, Baker blew out a breath.

Deepa Bhukari said, 'You've got to be kidding me.'

Rick and Akamu gave each other a fist bump.

And Agnes looked at Mavis, looked back at me and said, 'We're going to need a bigger crew.'

I fixed them with a grin. 'Let me guess; you know just the people to help out.'

Mr Tracksuit

Mr Tracksuit saw us coming, turned and fled the other way which drove him directly into Schneider and Pippin. Baker had recruited an additional two members of security. He wanted more but I not only insisted that we needed to keep the number of people involved to a minimum but also that I only wanted people I trusted and that was a short list.

Cornered, he put his hands up in surrender but smiled at us as if once again we had nothing on him. We were out on the eighteenth deck sun terrace where the sun beat down on the carefree holiday makers, either oblivious to or thus far unaffected by the potentially deadly disease waging war below decks. Many of them were sitting up on their loungers now, watching to see if anything interesting was going to happen.

'Again?' said Mr Tracksuit. 'Why don't you leave me alone?'

The question was aimed directly at me, but I didn't reply. I had a much better way to wipe the smile off his face. 'Amy?'

I saw his smile freeze at the name and fail completely when his diminutive girlfriend appeared from behind Schneider's back. 'Sorry, Max. They came to the cabin. They know everything.'

'Everything,' I echoed.

The everything we knew was that Max and Amy boarded the Aurelia in Vietnam. They were funding an around the world lifestyle by robbing anyone and everyone they could. In that, they were a lot like Agnes and Mavis but without the style and class. About a day after leaving Singapore where the two ladies had boarded, Max had picked a pocket right in front of Agnes just as she had been about to lift it herself. Impressed by his talent, they recruited him, forming an alliance that reduced the risk of getting caught while increasing the number of people they could target.

Amy stepped forward. 'It's okay, Max. They want us to help them.' His mouth formed a confused O shape, but his girlfriend took his hand to lead him away.

'So, we're off the hook with the pocket picking?' he asked.

Baker rolled his eyes. 'Yeah. We're even going to let you keep all the stolen stuff.'

Max turned to look at him. 'Really?' I decided at that point that Max wasn't very bright.

'No, not really,' answered Amy quietly. 'But they are not locking us up yet and if we help them it will go in our favour.'

'Oh. Okay. Well what do they want us to do?'

The answer to that took half an hour and a whiteboard to explain.

A Crazy Plan

Before we enacted the plan, I sent Deepa Bhukari to get Barbie; I needed her help with the makeup, and she knew the girls in the theatrical productions. Convincing the four security officers that this was the right plan took some doing too. They wanted to go directly to Acting Captain Shriver, but I argued I had already made contact and tried to explain. In my opinion, she was disinclined to listen but with the irrefutable evidence I planned to gather, the task of winning her over would be simple.

With our course of action settled, the entire troop decamped to my suite where Ramone gaped open mouthed at the odd assortment of friends traipsing in after me. Anna went nuts when I let her out of the bedroom, running and barking and generally trying to work out who it was she needed to kill first.

Barbie, the nimble little minx, deftly scooped her up for a hug and held her in the air as she sweet-talked her. 'She's such a funny little girl,' she said as she spun her around, then she stopped suddenly to stare out of my panoramic windows. 'Is that a warship?' she asked, pointing with an arm to make us all look.

Sure as anything, a large, grey battleship-looking thing was going by outside. Putting Anna down, since she had now calmed, Barbie went out through the patio doors to see it.

'It's a US Navy ship,' said Akamu, joining us at the railing. 'Now what would they be doing here?'

Lieutenant Schneider had the answer to that question. 'They are part of the US seventh fleet. Haven't you been keeping up with the news?' When a sea of blank faces stared back at him, he filled us in on current affairs. 'West Houptiou and East Houptiou have been at each other's throats since the West annexed itself twenty-five years ago. Open hostility hasn't broken out for many years, but the East has been noticeably building its military and would most likely invade if the West didn't have rich oil fields and a trade deal with America. The East threatened the US interest in this region, so the US seventh fleet is here to ensure the East doesn't do anything daft.'

'They can do that?' asked Amy.

Barbie grinned. 'It's the US Navy, honey. They can do anything.' Then she turned back toward the ship and gave them a whoop and a wave, jumping on the spot to get their attention. The passing ship was close enough for the sailors onboard to see there was a pretty blonde woman trying to get their attention so those on the deck started waving back. It was too far for the sound of voices to carry but when the bridge on the ship sounded its horn; the Navy warship equivalent of a wolf whistle, it was deafening.

The ship kept going, cruising along to wherever it was heading but there were other ships in the distance, their large, grey hulls easy to spot under the azure blue sky.

'Come on, gang.' I started flapping my arms to get everyone back inside. 'We need to get ready. There's a lot to do.' My motley crew filed back into the living area of the suite just as a knock came at the door.

Ramone opened it to reveal Baker and Pippin. They were pushing hospital beds, the same ones the orderlies were using and had piles of clothing on top of them. 'These were not easy to get,' said Baker.

They got them though and my crazy scheme was off and running.

I looked away from the beds to see that all eyes were on me. The team was waiting for instruction. 'Ok? Everyone knows their part, right? We just need to get makeup and change clothes and… hold on. Where's the crystal decanter gone?'

Everyone tracked where my eyes were staring. Everyone's except Agnes that is. On a low side table between two bookshelves had stood an ornate crystal decanter. It was suspiciously absent now.

When the eyes in the room tracked around to stare at her, Agnes just shrugged. 'Everyone's got to have a hobby.'

Baker shook his head in despair.

Mavis actually high-fived her. 'That was a slick move, girl. I didn't even see you take it.'

I took the offered decanter back and put it back on the table. They sure did have some skills, skills I needed to employ now. I clapped my hands again, this time to jolt people into action and a flurry of activity began.

Here's the thing about my plan; it was nuts. I mean, I couldn't have come up with a plan like this under any other circumstances and when I described it to the team it still sounded nuts to me even though I was convinced it would work.

I needed to get Dr Mendoza away from Dr Chouxiang and his team, that was task number one but if Dr Mendoza's family were being held hostage to make him cooperate, he would most likely refuse to come with me. He wanted help though, that much I was certain of, so I came up with a way to get him away from his captors and deter them from getting him back: We were going to fake his death.

How?

We were going to unleash a zombie attack in the sickbay.

I said it was nuts.

With Barbie's help, myself, Akamu, Rick and Mavis were transformed into living dead. She borrowed a huge box of makeup from a girlfriend and went to town adding weird effects that made our eyes look sunken and our cheeks pronounced. Our skin was going green and sloughing off in places. We were hideous. While that happened, Max, Amy, Agnes and Baker changed into the orderly's uniforms. They would push the hospital beds down to the sick bay and once inside, we would wake up and begin to attack. In the confusion, we would grab Dr Mendoza and escape with him.

Simple, huh?

Day of the Living Dead

Rick and Akamu looked to be having a great time, giggling at each other and joking. Rick asked Akamu when it was going to be his turn to get his make up done. Of course, it was already done but Rick was pretending his big friend looked no different. I felt like reminding them what was at stake, but I kept my mouth shut to focus on my own preparation.

Soon, we were loaded onto the hospital beds to start the journey down to the sick bay. I had butterflies but we were going through with this. Sheets went right over our heads so no one could see us in our horror makeup but also because we were supposed to be dead. I couldn't see anything of course, but I could hear gasps from passengers as we passed them. Light coming through the sheet changed in brightness as we moved away from the windows in the passageway and reached the elevator.

The ping of the elevator sounded, and I heard the doors swish open. Then there were more gasps as the people inside were confronted by four dead bodies covered by sheets.

Then Rick sneezed.

'What the heck?' someone said.

'That can happen,' Agnes replied, thinking clearly and quickly to cover up Rick's mistake which threatened to expose us all. 'The body continues to twitch for hours after death sometimes.'

'Eww, that's horrible,' said the woman.

'Oh, yes,' replied Agnes, really getting into character now. 'Did you know hair and nails continue to grow for up to two days after death and all the gases inside the body leak out by themselves for longer than that.'

Rick farted. It did a good job of emphasising the point about gas and we probably would have got away with it if Max hadn't giggled.

'Here, what's going on?' asked the woman.

'Yeah,' a man's voice. 'Who are you people? I'm calling security.'

I could feel the bed being rotated as Baker tried to reverse me into the elevator. It would fit all four of us, but the passengers outside were getting agitated and trying to stop us leaving until they could attract the attention of some crew members.

The little bell in the elevator was binging as the doors tried to close but something was stopping them. 'Can you move your foot please, sir? I have to get these bodies to sick bay.' Baker was trying to continue with our ruse, but no one was buying it anymore.

Knowing that I couldn't afford for the plan to fail, I threw back the sheet and sat up so the people outside the elevator could see my zombie appearance. Everyone was talking one second and silent the next. Then I opened my mouth to scream a guttural growl and the man with his foot in the door fell backward in fright.

The doors shut on a dozen stunned faces outside and we were away.

Baker hung his head. 'That was too close. They're going to report this, you know. Someone will be looking for us soon.'

'Then we had better get on with it, hadn't we?' I insisted. Then I turned my purse-lipped face to Max. He was sitting up on his bed and almost wetting himself at how funny it all was. When he saw my expression he soon shut up. 'That's better,' I snapped. 'Keep it that way. People's lives are at risk.'

I laid myself back down and had Baker arrange the sheet on top of me again. The elevator reached the tenth deck without anyone else trying to get on and we were mere yards from the sick bay. Nerves fluttered through my stomach again. Mostly this was to do with my concern over what Dr Chouxiang and his team were actually up to. This had to be some kind of criminal activity but what exactly? Were they smuggling drugs? Were they trying to infect the ship and create a diversion so they could rob it? The Aurelia was basically a floating palace so stealing cash, jewels, goods and other high value items might be lucrative. I thought it unlikely though, it was too much effort for not enough gain and too great of a risk with the disease loose on board. What was to stop them getting infected themselves?

Hold on. Why hadn't I asked that question before? How were they ensuring they didn't get infected? I didn't get to give it any thought though because Baker whispered that we had arrived, and I could hear the nurse on reception asking where we had been found.

Agnes supplied the concocted story and we were wheeled in. I knew from talking to Dr Kim that he wanted all the infected in one place. Having created a quarantine area, he didn't want anyone that died to be taken somewhere else because they didn't have anywhere else to take them. The ship's assigned sickbay was still treating normal complaints, so the only place we would wind up was in the sick bay with Dr Mendoza and Dr Kim and Dr Chouxiang and all the other doctors, fake or otherwise that were working this crisis.

As my bed rolled along, Baker continued to whisper to me, 'Dr Mendoza is treating a patient on the other side of the room. We've been directed to the far corner. I'm going to need to try to get him to come over.'

I whispered back, 'Okay,' and waited. The wait stretched out though. Baker left me to see Dr Mendoza, but treating and caring for the living took priority over dealing with the dead.

Bored with how long it was taking, I peeked out from under my sheet to get my bearings, gave Rick's bed a whack with my hand and said, 'Show time.'

Then I sat up. I did so slowly though, as if I was just coming to life, or unlife, or whatever the correct term is for zombies. We had practiced it in the room, going through a few jerky movements and trying to act like zombies because, well, who hasn't seen a zombie movie at some point?

Nothing happened for a few seconds, which wasn't how it was supposed to go. Amy was supposed to scream which would make everyone look just as whoever was nearest her started to fake bite her neck.

Barbie's makeup kit contained the gubbins to make fake blood so we each had a small bottle of that to spray around. The other people in the room wouldn't know to play along though so our ruse depended on us attacking our orderlies.

'Amy!' I hissed. It got her attention and as if suddenly remembering her lines, she screamed and Akamu grabbed hold of her.

The pandemonium in the sickbay was instant. Every head turned in our direction and most of them screamed as an automatic reaction to what they saw. Akamu had a limp Amy in his arms and was gnawing at her neck while using his squeezy bottle to shoot arcs of blood in the air.

It was convincing enough for me, but I had no time to watch the theatrics. I needed to get to Dr Mendoza. Like everyone else, his face was etched with petrified fear, but Dr Chouxiang Junior was standing next to him and he just looked angry. It was the first time I had seen Dr Mendoza without the elder brother in his shadow. I didn't know if that was a good or a bad thing, but I was in the act now and we had one shot to pull this off.

I growled an evil zombie growl and lurched toward Dr Mendoza. He didn't move, but Dr Chouxiang junior came straight for me. Right on cue, Agnes the orderly, running away from Mavis the zombie, ran straight into him, knocking him over in her haste to get away. She was screaming and flailing and fighting to get off him which distracted Dr Mendoza so he didn't see zombie Akamu come up behind him.

As Akamu grabbed the terrified doctor and held him in place, I converged on their position. 'Play along, this is a rescue,' I hissed as I pretended to bite his shoulder. I sprayed some blood on his shirt for good measure but the good doctor hadn't heard me.

He was still fighting to get away from Akamu, too terrified to listen and was in danger of wriggling free. He grabbed my hair and yanked at it painfully, so I did what I could and kneed him between the legs.

Then the doors burst open and white uniforms flooded in. Three of them with their firearms up and pointed at our heads. They opened fire into the crowd of people who were already screaming and running around. Shouts to, 'Get down!' convinced most people to hit the floor but Dr Chouxiang Junior was back on his feet after the double whammy of Mavis and Agnes and he wasn't fooled by any of our antics. Nor by the blanks Schneider, Pippin and Bhukari were firing. He could see me with Dr Mendoza and was coming right for me again.

I don't know if he recognised me through the makeup or not but I didn't get to ask him because Lieutenant Baker hit him over the head with a tray and knocked him out.

I swivelled Dr Mendoza toward the door and shouted, 'Time to go,' so everyone would hear me. Akamu and I had to pretty much carry Dr Mendoza from sickbay as he was trying very hard to curl into a ball. Between us, we got him outside as the rest of our team caught up with us.

In the passageway leading to sickbay the nurse who had been manning reception was nowhere to be seen and I exhaled a breath I seemed to have been holding for more than an hour. We were out and we had the doctor. It wasn't the clean getaway I wanted though. Dr Chouxiang hadn't believed the zombie attack for a second so my hope they would think him dead was crushed.

We had him though and that meant I could find out what was going on finally. With the three security officers in their white uniforms leading the way we got around the first corner. No one was following us, but both Rick and Akamu had been forced to move faster than normal and were out of breath so we paused for a second to gather ourselves.

I leaned Dr Mendoza against a bulkhead. 'Dr Mendoza, I know about your family. They are being held captive, aren't they?'

He blinked at me. 'You're the lady that returned my wallet. How do you know about my family?'

'I did some research and phoned your house. There is a person there impersonating your wife. I'm sorry, I couldn't confirm if your family were harmed or not.'

'They're not. They let me speak to them every day. It is the only way to get me to continue with this awful business.' Once again I saw the wretched look of despair on his face like he wanted to die right now and have it done with.

'Dr Mendoza, what is going on? You have to tell us everything right now,' I demanded. I felt like grabbing his collar and threatening him just to make him get on with it. I felt like blaming him for the sick people onboard but what would I do if my children were threatened? What would most people do?

'They are planning something on West Houpitou. Beyond that I don't know much. They grabbed me from my home ten days ago and had me take them to my research facility. They already had the cabins booked and everything prepared, they just needed me.'

'What for?'

'To get them a sample of Ebola,' he murmured, his eyes toward the deck as he admitted the awful truth.

'So, it is Ebola?' I confirmed.

He shook his head though. 'No, not anymore. They had a full laboratory waiting for me. They wanted something faster acting but also something treatable and preventable. Treatable so they could contain it should it spread beyond the borders of West Houptiou and preventable so they wouldn't get sick themselves.'

So that was why they were so unconcerned about their exposure. The big news was that it was treatable though. This time I did grab his shirt. 'Where is the cure, Dr Mendoza? Why aren't you treating the patients with it?'

His wretched face looked up at mine. 'Because they won't let me. They want to prove that what I created for them was deadly. They don't trust me, and I am going to have to go back to them now. They will kill my family.'

'We can help you with that,' I promised though I had no idea how to deliver. 'When we tell the captain, she will have the ship's security team grab the rest of Dr Chouxiang's team and coordinate with local authorities in Manilla to get your family freed.'

'You don't know these people,' he protested. 'Nothing will stop them. You can send the Army and the Navy, and it will make no difference. They have weapons with them in their cabins. I have seen them. They will fight and they are well trained.'

I didn't care for his defeatist attitude. 'I want that cure, Dr Mendoza. Where is it?'

'It's locked in their cabin, in a safe where you can't get to it. You don't even have a keycard to open the door.'

'Agnes,' I prompted.

Agnes held aloft Dr Chouxiang Junior's wallet. 'I also got his watch and a nice necklace. The watch is a Tag Heuer,' she boasted.

I could deal with her constant need to steal things later. 'Right now, we are going to their cabin and you are going to show me where the safe is.' I turned to look at the security officers. 'Any compunction about shooting these guys if they resist?'

Schneider fixed me with a determined look. 'If they are armed, we will deal with them.'

'How will you open the safe?' Dr Mendoza wailed.

I snorted a laugh at his question. 'Ladies?'

'Yeah, we can do safes,' replied Mavis without me needing to ask.

'I guess that's it then. Let's go.' I pushed the doctor toward Schneider. Dr Mendoza had recovered from the injury to his tender region and looked about ready to bolt. His faith in our ability to overcome the... what should I call them? I mentally settled on terrorists, so our ability to overcome the terrorists onboard was doubted by Dr Mendoza and that placed his family in jeopardy. I understood his feelings, but I wasn't going to allow his worry to cloud my judgment.

If things went the way I wanted, we could save everyone.

We reached the elevator and as we waited for the car to descend, my confidence grew and grew. We were going to win. I was going to save Alistair and Jermaine and all the other sick people on board.

Then the elevator pinged, and the door swished open to reveal a sight that stopped my heart. A dozen guns in the hands of the ship's white uniformed security team were pointing at us and Acting Captain Shriver was standing right in the middle of them.

That wasn't the worst bit though, for standing just behind her was the elder Dr Chouxiang.

The Brig

'Good afternoon, Mrs Fisher.' Acting Captain Shriver smiled at me in a satisfied way as if to say she knew she would catch me doing something ridiculous and now she had. 'I believe you wished to speak to me earlier. Was it so you could tell me a fanciful tale about Dr Chouxiang and his team?'

'They are terrorists,' I stated as clearly as I could.

'No, Mrs Fisher, they are renowned medical experts and are helping out with the virulent outbreak we have on board. They are doing so at their own risk of exposure and have been instrumental in assisting me to get the help we need. Even now there is a team in West Houptiou assembling supplies and additional medical professionals so they can bring this disease under control and treat those already infected. Isn't that right, Dr Chouxiang?'

'Indeed,' he replied with a knowing smile in my direction.

'They are not doing that at all,' I scoffed. 'Dr Mendoza is the world's leading authority on infectious diseases. They kidnapped him and have his family held captive. They forced him to concoct the deadly virus we now see infecting the passengers and crew of this ship and they intend to set it free on West Houptiou as a biological weapon because they cannot attack with military strength for fear the Americans will intervene.'

Acting Captain Shriver looked at Dr Mendoza, whose eyes, I noted, were locked on Dr Chouxiang's. Dr Mendoza was shaking with fear. 'Dr Mendoza, can you confirm what Mrs Fisher is saying?' she asked.

He swallowed hard, glanced at me with apologetic eyes and lied, 'I have no idea what she is talking about. I was doing my best to care for the patients when Mrs Fisher and her accomplices started a riot in the sickbay. It was terrifying. Not just for me, but for everyone in there. I really must get back to the patients as I fear her antics may have worsened the condition of those still alert enough to have witnessed it.'

'I think that about covers it,' Acting Captain Shriver said with a sneer. 'I would think it sufficiently condemning that we find you in the company of criminals the security team have been trying to locate. I shall assume they work for you.'

I opened my mouth to challenge her, but I knew there was no argument I could present that would work now. 'Commander Shriver,' I called to get her attention.

'That's Acting Captain Shriver,' she reminded me.

'Yes, Commander.' My reply angered her, but I didn't care. 'Your blindness will cost you and the people on board dearly.'

All she said in reply was, 'Take them away.' Pippin, Baker and the others were disarmed, and we were all searched for weapons and all under her watchful gaze. We weren't handcuffed or bound but under armed guard the eleven of us were escorted to the brig where, to my surprise, there were real cells with real bars.

We were processed efficiently, our personal effects removed and recorded, then placed into boxes and locked inside a large locker. We got to wash the makeup off and change into what were essentially prison clothes: jumpsuits and laceless overshoes. Then it was into the cells where maximum occupancy was twelve so we only just fit. 'What happens now?' asked Baker as the doors were locked.

Acting Captain Shriver had come all the way with us, determined to make sure we didn't manage to slip away or find new allies. 'You will remain here until we make port. At that point you will be handed over to the authorities. You should settle in and get comfortable. With the disease on board, I doubt we will be going anywhere for a while.' She turned to leave but paused at my cell to offer me a parting comment. 'Shame about your dear Captain Huntley. Still, out with the old and in with the new.' Her voice echoed back through the door as she walked away, happily whistling to herself.

The power of the big chair had gone to her head.

Two guards were left to watch over us, but when Baker and Schneider tried to talk sense into them, they closed the outer door and left us inside to stew.

For two hours there was almost no noise as we all stared at the walls and came to terms with our incarceration. There was no clock on the wall so I couldn't be exact about the time but it was stretching into forever when we heard noise outside for the first time since the door was closed on us.

'What now?' asked Bhukari. She was sitting on the floor with her back against the wall and her arms wrapped around her legs. None of my inmates had verbally assigned blame for their predicament to me but I felt guilty anyway. Guilty that we had been caught, not that we had attempted to help.

'Changing of the guard. Nothing to get excited about,' came Schneider's reply from the next cell.

I sighed and sat on the floor next to Deepa. We were arranged in three cells, five girls in one and two sets of three guys either side of us. There was a solid steel bulkhead dividing the cells so we couldn't see each other but we could talk.

'Anyone got a clever plan to get out of here?' I asked the air.

Max's snarky comment came back quickly. 'You're the brains of this outfit. You figure it out. You got us in here.'

Softly Amy said, 'That's not helpful, Max.'

'I wasn't trying to be helpful,' he snapped back at her.

I sat forward, arranging my thoughts. 'Look, we know they have a cure to treat the sick, but they are not using it. They also have weapons and are planning something terrible. Dr Chouxiang got to Commander Shriver first and has convinced her that he is the one that can help the sick. We have to get out of here and we have to stop them before they kill thousands or tens of thousands of people. It's up to us, there's no one coming to help us.'

Just then, the door opened, bringing all eyes up to see who was coming in. My jaw fell open when Barbie poked her head in. 'I thought you might need a jail break,' she said brightly.

I leapt to my feet and everyone else in my cell rushed to the bars to see.

'What happened to the guards?' asked Lieutenant Bhukari.

'They're, um, having a nap,' she said, her cheeks colouring in embarrassment. She looked at the lock on our door. 'There's no keyhole. How do I get it open?'

Next to me, Bhukari pointed to the desk. 'It's all electronic. You need to use the computer to deactivate the locks.'

Barbie settled into the chair and moved the mouse to bring it to life, fiddled for a bit while she chewed her bottom lip, then with a pop, the solenoids operated, and the doors all swung open together.

Just like that, we were out.

Baker and Schneider rushed to the doors and out. 'Hey, you tasered them!' Baker's voice echoed back. 'Nice move.'

Barbie grimaced. 'I did think about trying to seduce them but then couldn't work out how I would overpower them.'

'Where did you get the tasers?' Bhukari asked.

With a sly grin, Barbie said, 'I stole them from a couple of the guys a while back. Things keep getting dangerous around here. I thought they might come in handy.'

As they joked about it, I pulled open the locker and began handing out everyone's stuff. 'Alright, well we have to get moving. Guys,' I called to Baker and Schneider. When their heads appeared around the doorframe, I said, 'Can you drag them in here? We need to lock them up so they can't alert Shriver. From now on, we can't get caught.'

Rick tapped me on the shoulder. 'What are we going to do?'

'Funnily enough. I have a plan.'

Akamu put his head in his hands and wept. 'Of course you do.'

Uniforms and Disguises

Wearing prison clothes wasn't going to work. We needed to be invisible, so the security team put their uniforms back on and took the weapons from the two men Barbie tasered. Agnes, Max, Amy and Mavis put on the orderlies' outfits, it should ensure they blended in, even if two of them did look a little old for the role. Barbie was in her own clothes anyway. That left Rick, Akamu and me to fix up, but I had a plan for me.

'Deepa, switch clothes with me.'

'Hmm?'

'Take your uniform off again. I'm going to wear it. You won't need it because you are getting off the ship.'

Everyone looked at me like I was going a little nuts again. 'Why am I getting off the ship?'

'Better yet; how is she getting off the ship?' asked Schneider.

Sighing internally because I really didn't want to have to explain everything but understanding that they needed some guidance, I did my best to explain. 'If we pull this off and manage to get hold of the cure and defeat the terrorists, then what?' I got a lot of blanks looks.

'Surely we treat the sick with the cure?' asked Amy.

'Exactly,' I said and folded my arms because I thought my point had been made. The blanks looks continued though. 'Any of you know how much to give? How often? How to make more if we don't have enough? What temperature it needs to be kept at?' Now they were getting it. 'We might not need Dr Mendoza, but he is the one person we can guarantee has the answers to all those questions. Without him we could be wasting our time even getting hold of the cure, but his family are being held hostage and we have to arrange for them to be freed if we want him to help us.'

I turned to look at Deepa and Barbie. 'That's where you two gorgeous ladies come in.' They looked at each other. Barbie raised her hand. 'You don't have to raise your hand, sweetie,' I said as I pushed it down again.

'I still don't follow,' she said quietly like it was embarrassing to admit.

'Me neither,' said Deepa.

'Nor I,' added Schneider.

Baker nodded his head though. 'I think I know what she's got in mind.'

We locked eyes and said together, 'The jet skis.'

The ship caters for all sorts of activities, one of which is extreme water sports such as jet skiing, water skiing and water flyboard. A section of the ship on deck seven could be opened just above water level and a platform extended so guests could indulge in these activities when the ship was at anchor.

'We've got to get you there, but assuming we can, you two need to get to that US warship and get their attention. There's a US naval base in the Philippines, isn't there?'

Barbie nodded. 'Last time I checked.'

'Then your task is to convince them to send a team to free Dr Mendoza's family.'

'Can they do that?' she asked.

'You said they could do anything earlier. I think we need to put that to the test. Sorry, I wish I could come up with something else. This is my only play though.'

'Why those two?' asked Max. 'Why don't I go?'

Baker chuckled. 'If you were a US Navy ship filled with men, wouldn't you stop if these two popped up asking for a favour?'

Max stared at Barbie and Deepa. They were both very attractive women with great figures and ample bosoms. He stopped staring when Amy dug an elbow into his ribs. 'Yeah, well, I suppose, they do have certain… attributes that might help.'

'Plus, you're a scumbag criminal and I'm not letting you out of my sight,' added Baker. Conceding the point, Max fell quiet.

With that decided, Deepa and I exchanged clothes. Her uniform was more than a little snug on me, especially around my hips but I got it on and could still breathe. That just left Rick and Akamu.

'We could just wear the clothes we came down in,' offered Rick. He held up his shirt. It was blood soaked and had sticky zombie make up all around the collar. It needed to be burned not worn.

'How about their uniforms?' asked Barbie pointing to the two guards in their cells. They were awake and very sullen looking.

'Try it, cupcake,' one said with a sneer.

His partner had something to say too, 'Yeah, I owe you for tasering me. It's not going to get forgotten in a hurry, but I have a special way you can say sorry.' His creepy tone conveyed all that his words did not.

'Eww,' said Deepa. 'Don't you guys ever learn?' Then she tasered them both. This time using their own tasers which had been confiscated and left on the table next to her.

When they stopped twitching, Schneider unlocked the cells again and we stripped the two guards down to their underwear. It served them right for being unpleasant.

Akamu grimaced as he looked at himself in a mirror. 'We look a little old to be ship's security.'

Baker finished straightening Akamu's lapels. 'The intention is to not be seen. But when we approach anyone, just make sure you are at the back of the group and let Schneider or me do the talking.'

'Well, I think you look very handsome,' said Mavis, giving Akamu a pat on his rump that made him jump. She laughed playfully at him and he shot her a smile. I rolled my eyes. All this terror and being chased and the retirement aged people were flirting with each other.

'Ready?' I asked, some impatience in my voice quite deliberately.

Everyone nodded that they were, so with the two guards still yelling obscenities at us, my ragtag dozen set out to save the world. Or, at least, the bit of it on which we lived.

Splitting the Team

To make it easy for passengers to access, the ship's watersports activity centre was located midships and directly opposite one of the elevator banks. It was on the opposite side of the ship to the main entrance that most people came and went from when the ship docked anywhere which placed it close to water level with the ship fully laden. It could only be opened when the ship was at anchor, but it wasn't as easy as turning a handle.

The crew members got to work on preparing to open the door. There were a number of checks to carry out and a motor to engage and switches to throw and they were unfamiliar with the system. Only Barbie had used it before when she filled in for one of the instructors assigned to the watersports centre several months ago.

'You know this will activate a warning in the bridge, don't you?' said Schneider.

He was addressing the whole group, but I hadn't known that, and it hadn't occurred to me. 'What will they do?' asked Akamu.

Baker stopped what he was doing and leaned on an oversized valve thingy he was to operate. 'They will call down here to see if someone answers and dispatch a security detachment to investigate.'

Barbie looked concerned. 'How long will we have from when the alarm sounds?'

Baker and Schneider exchanged a glance. 'Maybe ten minutes,' Baker replied with a worried look. 'But it will start to sound the moment we engage the motor and it will take about ten minutes to get the door open from that point.'

'How many will they send?' I asked.

Again Baker answered, 'Probably four. Or, perhaps I should say, typically four, with all that is happening, they might send everyone.'

'Then we need a diversion,' said Rick, levering himself off the jet ski he was resting on. 'Akamu and I can take care of that. If they have more than one thing to deal with, they will have to divide their forces. If they have three things, they will need to spread themselves even thinner.'

I nodded; it was a solid idea. 'What will you do?'

Rick shrugged. 'Something inventive.' Akamu clapped his friend on the shoulder and they headed back to the door; two friends embroiled in an insane adventure.

'Meet us on the eighteenth deck,' I called after them. 'We need to get the cure next.'

Barbie confirmed that everyone was ready and they started the process of opening the sea door. We couldn't see it, but I had to assume that up on the bridge a little light was flashing or an alarm of some kind was bleeping. The person looking at it would tap the screen or maybe make a call and then they would call down to the phone in the watersports place to see if anyone was in here. That would take them at least a couple of minutes, right?

The phone rang. It had been about four seconds.

The only people not doing anything were Max and Amy, who were too young and dumb to be allowed to answer it and Mavis and Agnes who would probably steal it and the watch from the person at the other end.

I answered it instead. 'Watersports centre, Lieutenant, um, Fisher, speaking.'

'This is Ensign Willborough on the bridge. I'm showing the sea door opening on my monitor. What are you doing in there?'

I hadn't thought about this bit so I had no lie lined up to deliver. 'We, ah, we had some passengers that wanted to use the jet skis. They were fed up with being on the ship at anchor.' I winced at how pathetic that sounded.

Just then, there was a whump noise as a small explosion happened not very far away. Instantly, I could hear an alarm warbling at the other end of the phone. 'Hold on,' shouted Ensign Willborough. 'There's a fire near you. I'm sending a team to tackle it.'

'There's no need really, we can deal with it.'

'I thought you had passengers with you. Your priority has to be their safety. Give me your rank and name again.'

I hung up the phone. 'We're going to have company,' I yelled. The door was already partway open, and I saw the flaw in Baker's calculation. It would take ten minutes to get the door fully open, but we only needed an aperture of about three feet to get the jet skis through.

Agnes saw it too. 'Quick, Mav, grab that end.' They started wheeling one of the jet skis to the door on its little trailer.

Barbie was engrossed in operating the motor that opened the door and hadn't realised she could stop already. I gave her a hug and pointed. 'Good luck. We're going to try to get the cure anyway. That might endanger Dr Mendoza's family.'

I wasn't sure what I was trying to say, but Barbie grabbed my hands to stop me wringing them. 'I'll be fine,' she reassured me, picking up that I was gabbling because I was nervous about her. 'Go get the cure. Treat

Jermaine and the captain and everyone else and I will be back with Deepa before you know it.'

I nodded, worried despite her confidence. Lieutenant Deepa Bhukari was already at the door and astride a jet ski. 'Come on, Barbie, let's get going.' As I watched, Baker and Schneider lifted the frame her jet ski was resting on and it slid free to drop two feet to the water.

Barbie and I hugged again quickly then she took a run and dived out the door just before the second jet ski was tipped out the door to splash in the water. I got to the door just in time to see both girls fire up the engines and rocket away from the ship.

'Rick started a fire,' moaned Akamu from behind us.

We turned to find both men looking a little singed. Their white uniforms were no longer pristine as they now had soot marks on them which extended onto their faces. I laughed. I couldn't help myself. There was no time for mirth though, we had to get out of the area before anyone else turned up. We had two weapons between the ten of us and that wasn't enough to do anything with. Plus, none of us wanted to be shooting at other members of the crew. We would all be on the same side again when this was done.

With the girls gone, we were hanging around for no good reason, and everyone knew it, so without any prompting, everyone started heading for the elevator.

Rick leaned against the wall by the call button. 'An elevator. Thank goodness. I can't keep running about like this.'

Baker shook his head. 'They'll come that way. We need to take the stairs.'

Rick shot him a dirty look. 'Ah, nuts.'

Cure

Thankfully, we didn't need to take the stairs very far. Baker led us up one flight, which was quite enough for the older men, and then along a long passageway to a different elevator. We were in a part of the ship that had no entertainment so there were no people around. There were cabins but it was a time of the day when people would be by the pool or off doing something.

This suited us. We had looked ridiculous as a group before but with Rick and Akamu's newly blackened uniform's we stood out. Before, from a distance I was content that we probably wouldn't get a second glance. Now though, it was easy to spot that we didn't belong.

Unfortunately, we had to negotiate our way to Dr Mendoza's cabin and on deck eighteen there were pools and restaurants and shops and other activities. The passageway would be filled with passengers and crew. Lots and lots of them. There was no way around it and when the elevator doors opened, there were people in front of us straight away.

I felt panic rising but as we got off, they got on, too busy with their own lives to pay us any attention. I let my held breath go and Schneider clapped me on the shoulder. 'You worry too much, Mrs Fisher. We should split up into smaller groups though. We'll be less conspicuous that way.'

The real issue was that Rick and Akamu just didn't look right in their uniforms. Someone was going to spot them and know something was amiss and the chance of running into other crew members was very high, so they elected to strip off their top halves. Walking around inside the ship with nothing on one's top half was discouraged but at worst a member of crew would have a discrete word with them.

Broken into smaller groups we were able to get to Dr Mendoza's cabin unchallenged and by the time I got to the door, Mavis already had it open. The keycard from Dr Chouxiang Junior's wallet proved useful, though I wouldn't have been shocked if the two women had been able to open the door without it.

We planned for Baker and Schneider to go in first. They were armed and we had to be prepared for one of the terrorists to be inside. Incredibly, the cabin was empty, but I saw instantly that the safe was too.

Mavis had her hands on her hips and a bored expression. 'I was looking forward to opening that.'

'Search the place,' I instructed, going back to the door to usher the final group inside. At the rear, as always, were Rick and Akamu, they were with Agnes and somehow they both had brand new shirts on now. I could see the packet creases on them still.

They saw me looking at them. 'Agnes swiped them,' Rick explained.

'You're welcome,' she called out as she joined the others in tossing the cabin.

I folded my arms and stared at the two ex-cops. Akamu had the decency to look guilty. 'She just appeared with them. We were drawing attention with our manly physiques and it was too late to take them back by the time she handed them to us. It would have drawn too much attention going back into the shop with stolen goods.'

He was right, but that was hardly the point. Bigger fish to fry, I told myself.

Pippin came through from the bedroom to find me. 'Mrs Fisher, you have to see this.'

We all followed him back through the door where, on the bed, Baker and Schneider were staring at suitcases. 'What've you got, gentlemen?'

Baker gave me a grim look. 'Dr Mendoza said they were armed.' He took a pace to one side so I could see the contents of the suitcases. They were empty, but what they used to have in them were machine guns or assault rifles. I wasn't sure exactly but the suitcases had foam inserts to conceal dozens of guns. 'He wasn't kidding,' Baker added, his voice filled with concern.

As the significance of the find hit me, I slumped against the wall. 'If they have taken the guns and the cure, they are planning to leave. They must be. Shriver said they made contact with a team of disease control specialists in West Houptiou. Whoever that is, they are sailing into an ambush. When they arrive, Dr Chouxiang and his team are going to overpower them, load the disease, the cure, and the vaccine aboard and take the craft back to West Houptiou posing as the team that just left there. No one will know the difference.'

'Oh, my life.' Schneider shook his head. 'It's brilliant. They can waltz right into the country with a deadly biological weapon and release it in cities and towns, infecting the whole country and there will be no one to stop them.

Rick punched the wall for emphasis. 'Unless we stop them, dammit.'

'This isn't compulsory, is it?' asked Max. He was hugging Amy and they both looked scared. 'I'm just a guy that's good at swiping stuff that's not mine. No one said anything about getting into a gun battle with terrorists over a biological weapon that can kill everyone.'

Rick sneered at him. 'I spent my life chasing after punks like you. All you do is take, well, now someone's asking you to give back. If we don't stop them, they escape with the cure and the vaccine to leave us stuck onboard a ship with the deadly disease. How do you think we'll get on then?'

Rick was right. But this wasn't a job for Max and Amy, or me for that matter. We were not trained for such tasks. Going head to head with armed terrorists was beyond my capabilities. But maybe we could force Shriver to listen this time.

Baker threw his gun on the bed. 'We can't tackle them alone, Mrs Fisher. Schneider and I have got thirty bullets between us. We need help. What do we do?'

I gave everyone in the room a solemn look. 'We surrender.'

Surrender

It was a crazy thing to do, given the effort we went to getting this far, but the guys were right; we couldn't win without more firepower. There was no need for the whole team to be involved though. Rick and Akamu had been through a lot already and were starting to show signs of strain.

Just before I dealt with them and the others, I said, 'Lieutenant Baker please make the call to bring Shriver to us. She needs to see the weapons cases. If this doesn't convince her, I don't know what will.' Rick and Akamu had found chairs to rest on in the abandoned main living space of the cabin. With them at the table were Agnes and Mavis. 'Listen,' I said as I got their attention, 'you should head back to your cabins. The only thing left to do now is head off the terrorists before they escape. We'll have to move fast for that but it's really a job for the security team so the rest of us should leave it to them.'

'So, we're free to go?' asked Max, one foot already twitching toward the door. Baker shot me a look, but I shrugged. 'It's not like they can get off and escape.' To Max and Amy, I said, 'If you want to go, this is your chance. Your crimes are not forgiven but no one is going to put you in the middle of a gun battle if that's what this comes down to.' He needed no further prompting. With Amy's hand in his, they raced through the door and vanished.

'They're coming,' announced Baker. 'Shriver was a little shocked to hear my voice. They hadn't noticed our escape from the brig yet.'

I looked back down at the four people sat around the table. All were in their sixties or seventies but none of them were moving. If they wanted to sit this one out, they were running out of time to leave. Then I noticed the hands being held under the table. Mavis and Akamu and Rick with Agnes.

Agnes looked up at me. 'I think its time we stood for something.'

Mavis patted her friend's arm with her free hand. 'Yeah, I'm tired of being on the run all the time. I want to live somewhere and feel better about myself.'

'We're going to see this one through to the end,' added Rick. 'Then we'll see where that leaves us. There's no bench for us to sit this one out on. It's like you said; we stop them or we probably all get infected.'

All I could do was nod, but Baker had other thoughts on the matter. 'Is this romance blossoming? Are we planning to sail into the sunset together? Are we not forgetting the decades of crime the ladies need to answer for and all the passengers on board this very ship they have stolen from?'

No further discussion was possible because the sound of running boots in the passageway outside announced the security team heading our way. Baker and Schneider brought the gun cases out to the front of the cabin and we waited.

It sounded like a lot of boots coming our way and it was. They began spilling through the doorway, their guns up and ready but it wasn't their usual handguns, this time they held larger automatic weapons, the type a ship might have to repel pirates. The faces behind them looked mean.

'Drop your weapons,' the lead man shouted.

Calmly Baker looked at the hands we all held aloft. 'We don't have any weapons. Just the two handguns you can see on the carpet by my feet. Where is Commander Shriver?'

'Captain Shriver is on the bridge where the captain belongs. She can direct our efforts from there.'

'Captain Shriver?' I asked. 'Has she promoted herself already?'

Ignoring me, Baker softened his voice, 'Commander Pace.' He waited until he had the man's attention and started again. 'Mike, look at the suitcases. This is the cabin the team of doctors now helping Shriver were staying in. We think they're from East Houptiou. The infection on board - they brought that with them, and they are going to release it on a civilian population in West Houptiou if we don't stop them.'

Commander Pace licked his lips, a nervous gesture, and glanced about the room.

'Where is Dr Chouxiang now?' I asked. 'Is he still on the bridge? Or did he head down to meet the ship from West Houptiou already?' I saw doubt flicker across the commander's face. 'He did, didn't he?'

My arms were getting tired above my head, so I dropped them back to my sides. All the guns flickered in my direction. 'Shriver's gone nuts. You know it as well as the rest of us. The man she is taking advice from is a terrorist. He has the cure for the disease, he has the disease itself and he is heavily armed.' I indicated the empty suitcases with the gun shaped holes.

Schneider chipped in. 'If we don't stop them, they will get off this ship and take the cure with them. There is no other cure for the disease. If we let it go with them, everyone on board will get infected.'

Baker dropped his hands too, and all the weapons twitched once more. 'I'm going to reach down and pick up my gun.'

'Don't do it,' warned Commander Pace.

'I'm going to try to stop the terrorists we have been harbouring and see if I cannot save everyone on board. If you have to shoot me, then shoot me, but I would rather that than the slow death the people in the sick bay are suffering.' Slowly Baker began to crouch down toward the handguns by his feet.

A young female lieutenant standing next to Commander Pace risked a glance at her superior. 'Sir?' It was a question laced with multiple questions, but as Baker's hand neared his weapon, I saw the commander's grip tighten on his own gun.

Then his radio crackled and Shriver's voice cut through the silence. 'Commander Pace, report. Are the criminals in custody?'

Everyone froze as he reached up to touch his radio. 'Not yet, ma'am. Ma'am, they are saying the medical team are heading to the mainland with the disease and plan to release it there.'

'Of course that's what they are saying, you moron. I want them in custody, do you understand?'

'But, ma'am, there are weapo…'

She cut him off with an angry shout, 'I don't care what evidence you think you can see. I will not have insubordination. I am the captain of this ship and you will obey my orders without question.'

Commander Pace's finger hovered over the radio send button once more, but then moved slightly and hit the off switch instead. 'I really don't like her,' he said as he lowered his weapon. 'Alistair Huntley's still the captain of my ship. Let's get that cure and save him.'

I huffed out a sigh of relief, feeling the deck spin beneath my feet as my whole body sagged. At the table, the four occupants rested their heads in their hands and even Baker's shoulder drooped in relief. Then he snatched up the two handguns and threw one to Schneider.

'We have to move,' said Baker, heading for the door to force those currently stuffed into it out of his way. 'How long ago did Dr Chouxiang leave the bridge?'

Commander Pace checked his watch. 'Maybe fifteen minutes.'

Fifteen minutes. They had a fifteen-minute head start. That was too long.

'We sent a team with them,' Commander Pace said suddenly, switching his radio on and trying to raise them. As a single body, we were heading for the elevators. Shocked passengers diving into doorways and back down side passageways to get out of the way of the armed hoard. Rick and Akamu were bringing up the rear, shuffling along as best they could.

'Anything?' asked Schneider.

Commander Pace shook his head. 'No answer. I'm going to take that as a bad sign.'

I tapped Commander Pace on his arm. 'How far away is the team coming from West Houptiou?'

We reached the elevators, scattering passengers queuing there. Commander Pace sucked on his teeth. 'I'm not sure. They were on their way. They could be here already. The team we sent with them included deck hands to open the sea door on the eighth deck.' I knew the door he was talking about. It was one deck above the main door to the ship and had an extending platform. Unlike the watersports centre which opened almost directly onto the water and was sealed so any water coming in wouldn't flood the ship, the main door on deck seven, the one used to load and offload passengers, had no such protection so couldn't be used safely at anchor.

I hadn't done a head count but with the eight left from my crew there had to be nearly thirty of us, more than half of them heavily armed and hopefully well trained. Looking about though, a sense of absolute dread stole over me. Things happened so fast that I had allowed myself to be swept along with them, never questioning if I should take myself to one side. I'm a middle-aged woman with no fighting skill or knowledge of weapons, what the heck was I doing here?

Too late, the elevator pinged its arrival at deck eight, and the doors swished open.

Then the shooting started. The instant the elevator doors were open, a rear guard or whatever you want to call it, opened fire on us. I guess Dr Chouxiang had left a team to watch their backs in case anyone followed, and they were ready for us.

The shots went high, gouging the steelwork of the elevator car above our heads and in a panic, the security team burst outwards, running for cover while returning fire. I got carried along with them, losing sight of Rick, Akamu, and anyone else I knew.

'Throw down your weapons!' ordered Commander Pace.

His answer came back in the form of bullets followed by a scream of, 'East Houptiou forever!'

Pinned as we were in the small passageway in front of the elevators, we couldn't advance but we could go around. I didn't see much of the battle because I was cowering in a doorway, but Baker and Schneider, leading three other crew ducked down the stairs next to the elevator to reappear on the other side of the terrorists. Now fighting two fronts, they were unable to keep everyone's head down and were picked off, surrendering when it was clear they would die if they fought on any longer.

Pace left men behind to secure them and crept further toward the sea door, leading his team to an uncertain future. I couldn't help but tag along. I wanted that cure.

'Patricia,' hissed Akamu. He had snuck up next to me. He was out of breath and looking flushed, but he had something for me. It was a machine gun.

'Oh, my life, no!' I exclaimed, pushing it away. 'Wherever did you get that?'

'A couple of the security team got hit and stayed behind. It means their numbers are depleted. Rick and I are going to do our bit. If we can keep up, that is.'

What he said made sense. I didn't want the gun though. I couldn't imagine using it. I could put no further thought to my choices though because we had arrived.

Pace and Baker were standing either side of a closed bulkhead door. The wide expanse of the sea door bay was on the other side of it and they were counting down to time their attack. Baker had one hand in the air with three fingers held aloft for everyone to see. Three, two, one, and they yanked the door open.

Brave men and women of the Aurelia's security team began funnelling swiftly through the bulkhead door to fan out on the other side. I couldn't see anything, but when no one opened fire I was both relieved and dismayed. No one was getting shot at but surely it meant Dr Chouxiang and his team had already left.

I peered through the legs of the next man through the door just as the shooting started again. In the confines of the passageway, it was deafening and my ears were still ringing from the first firefight.

Bullets struck the steel of the bulkhead by my head, deforming it but not penetrating; I was safe where I was. However, I was soon the only person still this side of the door. Then the shooting stopped.

I risked a glance through the doorway to see what was happening.

It was a stalemate. The small medical supply vessel had docked alongside the Aurelia. It was tied off to secure it but once that task was done the terrorists must have produced their weapons and overpowered the medical team from West Houptiou. It didn't look like they had offered any resistance as I could see half a dozen or more of them being used as human shields right now. Dr Chouxiang had a gun to one woman's head, the threat obvious: stand down or we shoot the hostages.

The commander's training didn't allow for this. No one's did. We couldn't let them get away with the vaccine and the cure, but we couldn't sacrifice the hostages either. The delay he caused was all Dr Chouxiang needed though.

Still hiding behind their human shields, the terrorists shot out the lines tying the medical supply ship to the Aurelia and it slipped free.

I darted forward. 'No!' I cried. 'We can't let them get away!'

It was too late though, as the smaller vessel drifted clear, the engine caught with a determined buzz and it sprang forward. Dr Chouxiang shouted something in his native tongue and in response all the hostages were thrown into the water. If we had a chance to fire on them now, they were ready for it, for they unleashed a barrage into the sea door's aperture with everything they had, keeping heads down and minimising the shots fired back at them.

The crew from the medical supply ship were being swept away on the tide, the Aurelia's crew reacting to try to save them. I just stared at the back of the boat as it sped away from us. The cure was gone and there was nothing I could do to save Alistair or Jermaine or anyone else.

Feeling lost, I slumped to the deck.

What Women Can Achieve

A shout brought my head back up. Something was happening outside on the water.

'Mrs Fisher! You need to see this!' shouted Pippin excitedly. 'You're not going to believe it.'

I scrambled to my feet, getting them back under me so I could run to the edge of the sea door to see what everyone else was looking at.

The medical supply ship with the terrorists on board was still moving away from us but it was beginning to veer off its course as something emerged from the ocean to block its path.

'That's a submarine!' someone yelled, unable to mask the triumphant tone in their voice.

Whoever said it was right too. An enormous leviathan was pushing the surface out of its way as first its nose and then its conning tower sprang from the sea. It was huge. Not as big as the Aurelia of course but it bristled with implied threat and was blocking the path of the tiny medical supply vessel by its sheer broadside length.

Then hatches began to pop open as men in uniform scrambled from the mighty grey submarine. They were US Marines, armed to the teeth and trained to kill if necessary.

The terrorists steered their ship away, heading for the stern so they could slip around it as the sub continued forward. Shots were exchanged, Marines laying down a barrage of fire to pepper the smaller ship. It didn't slow them though and the submarine was still moving forward. Soon the terrorists would be able to get around them and escape.

I didn't give the Marines enough credit though, they had launches in the water and a team were erecting a far larger gun on the rear deck. The sound of the heavy calibre machine gun carried across the water and we could see it churning up the waves in front of the terrorist's ship. They were deliberately aiming to miss them; the Marines knew not to sink it.

I wondered how they could be so well informed but a whoop told me the answer. I swung my gaze around to look at the conning tower and there was Barbie and Deepa, easy to pick out because they were the only women visible and were waving madly at everyone on the Aurelia.

Barbie had a loudhailer. 'Hey, Patty! I found some sailors!' she laughed deeply as both she and Deepa high-fived half a dozen men in the conning tower with them.

I shook my head in disbelief.

With the loudhailer back at her mouth, Barbie shouted, 'They're sending a team to get Dr Mendoza's family too.'

Someone slapped me on the back, and I turned to see that it was Baker. He was the first but soon everyone wanted a go at congratulating me. It felt wrong. All I had done was stumble over a stolen wallet. No one was listening though. They were hailing me a hero and saying I had saved the ship.

The task wasn't done yet though. Amid the handshakes and high-fives, I shouted over the din, 'We still need to get the cure. There are people to treat and I don't know where Dr Mendoza is.'

A fresh exchange of bullets in the distance brought our focus back to the terrorists on the medical supply ship. The Marines were boarding but not without some last vestiges of resistance. It was over though, and I just hoped the cure was still intact.

The next half an hour was another flurry of activity. The US Navy frigate we saw earlier returned to lend more help and we welcomed aboard the Executive Officer of the submarine, Commander Steve Krill. He led a contingent of US Marines and sailors plus the full complement of the sub's medical staff.

'I believe I need to hand this to a Mrs Fisher,' he said as he held aloft a sealed titanium container. It was roughly the size of a case of wine but had a biohazard symbol on it. Beneath the warning symbols was the word cure in crudely written permanent marker.

Commander Pace greeted the visiting submarine crew as the senior officer in the sea door area, but he swung his attention to me now. 'This is Mrs Fisher.'

Commander Krill came forward, tucked the box under his left arm and snapped out a crisp salute with his right. 'Ma'am, I believe we owe you a debt of gratitude. Had the other box,' he indicated a Marine carrying a similar container, 'reached the shore. Well... I hate to think what might have happened. So strange to think the might of the US Navy could be defeated by something so small.'

I wasn't sure what to say. I felt as if I should stand to attention or something. Baker stepped forward to take the container from Commander Krill and I put my hand out for him to shake. 'Thank you, Commander, for coming to our rescue. However did the girls find you beneath the waves?'

'My sonar man heard the small engines from their jet skis. We are patrolling a no sail zone so went to investigate. The captain expected to find an incursion team from East Houptiou trying to get to shore so we were a little surprised to find two rather lovely gals skipping over the waves in their underwear. They were miles offshore and heading out to sea so we... offered them a lift.'

Of course Barbie had stripped off. What better way to attract the Navy, than by showing a little flesh?

'Patty!' her yell drew my attention and Commander Krill's too as she bounded across the deck to get to me. A fresh boat had arrived from the submarine carrying her and Deepa with it.

Barbie swept me up into a hug. 'Patty, that was so much fun! Let's never do that again.'

I laughed. It was genuinely funny. After all the terror and horror and shooting, Barbie said something funny and all I could do was laugh. She laughed too and soon everyone was joining in.

We had won. But only if the cure worked would it feel like a victory. 'We have to get to sick bay.' I grabbed her hand as I started moving. Tugging her along behind me, I all but ran back to the elevator. The cure had gone ahead of us, but I still didn't know where Dr Mendoza was.

I arrived at the makeshift sickbay a few minutes later, coming through the doors with my eyes wide in the hope I would spot Dr Mendoza among the medical staff crowding excitedly around the container with the cure in it.

He wasn't anywhere in sight though. Dr Kim, looking haggard and with a two-day stubble, was trying to organise the sudden influx of help all looking to be productive. The team from the submarine included two doctors and they brought with them a dozen other trained personnel and supplies of plasma and other drugs. Even as I watched, fresh IV drips were being hung.

There was nothing I could do to help. There were enough people in the room already and no doubt more coming as the frigate loaned its medical facility to the rescue effort. Slipping my hand from Barbie's, I found Alistair. He was still in his bed and looking deathly pale. I touched his face, but he didn't react. He looked weak and like all the other patients his skin was coated in a sheen of perspiration.

Barbie joined me, touching my arm gently as she leaned in. 'Jermaine looks the same.'

Neither of us had anything further to say. We both hoped for a swift recovery, but they looked so ill I wasn't sure what to expect. I could hear Dr Kim and the other doctors discussing dosing and fussing because they didn't know what to do. Too much, one argued, and it might be just as deadly as none at all.

Where was Doctor Mendoza?

The answer came to me in that instant. 'He's with the terrorists!' I blurted loud enough for the doctors and medical staff to swing their eyes in my direction. 'Dr Mendoza. He crafted the disease, the vaccine, and the cure. He is the only one that knows how to administer it correctly. Dr Chouxiang will have taken him with them so the Marines must have him in custody now.'

'Surely he would have protested his innocence,' argued Barbie.

'He probably did, but why would anyone listen to him. To the Marines, he's just another terrorist guilty by association because he's on a boat with a team of terrorists.'

One of the US Navy doctors was on his radio already, speaking with someone at the submarine. 'They've been transferred to the frigate already. They are sending someone to locate him.'

We waited with bated breath for more than ten minutes until his radio crackled again and the report came through that they had him. The Marines had treated all the terrorists on the boat equally, assuming they were all one team. For the Marines' safety, once disarmed the terrorists were cuffed and gagged so Dr Mendoza had no opportunity to identify himself. He was free now though and would be heading over to us as soon as they could ready a boat.

I slumped against Alistair's bed. Perhaps now we stood a chance.

Now that they didn't need to fight over how to dispense the cure, the doctors and other staff set about checking on the sick and tending to their needs. Barbie and I were ushered out of the way along with anyone else deemed nonessential.

'What do we do now, Patty?' asked Barbie as we walked hand in hand back to the elevators.

I was bone tired. All I wanted to do was sleep but I doubted I could until I knew my friends would be alright. 'I think I'm just going to head back to my room. Little Anna has been locked up in there for hours now. Ramone won't have let her out because she keeps attacking him.'

'Okay, Patty. I might go for a workout,' she replied, rolling her shoulders and twisting her hips while we waited for the elevator. 'I have nervous energy to burn off. Would you like to join me?'

'You can get stuffed.'

Barbie burst out laughing. 'Patty, you are so funny.'

We rode up in the elevator together though, both getting off on the top deck. Outside the door to my suite, she gave me a hug and carried on to the gym.

I patted my pockets until I found my door card, swiped the door and pushed my way inside.

Boy was I looking forward to getting Deepa's uniform off. It had been squashing my belly for too long. And I needed a gin and tonic, like literally more than I needed oxygen, such was my need for a drink.

The unmistakeable click of a safety catch being released stopped me short.

Dr Chouxiang

I froze at the sound, my heart instantly hammering in my chest though I dared not turn around to see who was behind me.

The hard muzzle of a gun poked into the back of my skull painfully. 'Hello, Mrs Fisher,' said the unmistakably unpleasant voice of Dr Chouxiang Junior. 'You should not have meddled in our affairs.'

'Why aren't you with the others?' I enquired.

He shoved the back of my head with the gun again. 'Move.' It was a simple instruction and I had no choice other than to comply as he forced me through from my suite's entrance lobby to the main living area. There was no sign of Ramone but that could mean his murdered body was hidden behind the kitchen units or that he just wasn't here. I hoped it was the latter.

'Why did you do it?' I asked, trying to get him talking so I could prolong this until someone came to rescue me. 'Why would you want to infect all those innocent people?'

He spat on my carpet. 'Innocent people? West Houptiou has no innocent people. They are all guilty. They took our mineral wealth when they split up the country. I was but a boy when the war started but my father remembered. He remembered prosperity and food on the table. Our mother died when the first bombs landed.'

'But your doctor's oath; first do no harm.'

'I am not a doctor, you stupid woman. Neither is my brother. We both trained in the East Houptiou military, advancing to special forces and then to covert ops. The plan to destroy our enemy with a biological weapon was his master stroke. I am sad that I will not get to see his plan succeed.

He wanted me to come with him to West Houptiou but I defied him so I could kill you. I knew you had worked it out. When you brought that ridiculous fake zombie attack into the sickbay and stole my wallet, I knew then that you were going to ruin our plans. My brother got away though, didn't he? Even now he is docking in West Houptiou and will deliver my revenge for me.

I locked eyes with him. 'No. Actually, he isn't. If you were on the other side of the ship, you would have seen the US Navy intercept his boat.' I tried to keep the triumphant gloating from my voice, but I didn't do a very good job.

'You lie!' he roared.

'Do I?

He backed off a pace, pointing his gun at my head again. 'Whether you are telling the truth or not,' he said calmly, 'it is now time for you to die, Mrs Fisher. I would like to prolong your death, string it out for a few days yet, but I doubt very much that we will remain undisturbed for that length of time...'

He continued to drone on about what he wanted to do to me, but I wasn't listening to him anymore. From the corner of my eye I had spotted an incongruity. The priceless crystal decanter was missing again. It was there when we left, I was certain of it. After Agnes swiped it, I put it back and I had been the last one from the room. Had Ramone moved it for cleaning?

Annoyed, the fake Dr Chouxiang snapped his fingers to get my attention. Bringing my focus back to the maniac standing before me I asked, 'I'm sorry what were you saying?'

'Any last requests?' he repeated.

'I suppose asking you to shoot yourself won't work?' The question actually brought a wry smile to his face, but he brought the gun up to point to my head again anyway. 'I want my husband's photograph,' I blurted. When he frowned, I added, 'He died last year. I keep his picture by my bed. I want to hold that next to my heart when… when you do it.'

He pursed his lips in impatience but nodded his head. 'Don't try anything, Mrs Fisher. There's nowhere to go and no one is coming to save you. If you make a sudden move, I'll shoot you in the head and be done with it.'

My pulse hammered so hard I could barely hear but walking to my bedroom door, slowly and deliberately so he wouldn't suspect anything, I glanced around the room. I was trying to find the one thing that might get me out of here.

'Stop.'

I stopped.

'This is your bedroom?' he asked while pointing at the door with his gun. When I nodded, he put six bullets through the door at chest height. I covered my ears quickly but took them away when he finished and pointed the weapon back at me. 'I don't trust you, Mrs Fisher. You are too wily, so if you had a man behind the door, I doubt he is coming to your rescue now.'

With an oh-so-clever smile he reached forward and opened the door.

Anna attacked him on sight. Five inches tall and full of pent up anger, she flew at his feet. I tried to go for his gun as the tiny attack dog caught him by surprise, but he jumped back in shock and fired a burst into the carpet.

He missed Anna but hit his own foot. Now howling in anger and pain, he had Anna tearing at the ankle of his uninjured leg and was hopping on it to save using the one with a hole in it.

I lunged for the gun again, but he levelled it back at me before I could get to him and once again, he was in control.

His face was a mask of pain when he sneered at me, 'Nice try, Mrs Fisher. Is that your final gambit?'

When I smiled in return, his expression changed from victory to concern. 'Not quite.'

I saw his finger begin to tighten on the trigger, but the crystal decanter smashed over his head before he could get the shot off. He lost consciousness and slumped to the floor, revealing Max's stunned face behind him.

I collapsed back into a chair wondering what might happen next. Max wasn't moving. 'You're a rubbish thief, you know that, Max.'

Max though, was watching Anna. 'Is that normal?' he asked.

I glanced at my dog. She had switched from terrorising his trousers and was now humping his foot in what looked like a display of dominance. I let her get on with it.

Jermaine

'Two ice cubes, madam?'

'Yes, thank you.' I heard two ice cubes clink into my glass and the sound of liquid being poured over them. I was sitting on my private terrace with Jermaine on the sun bed next to me and Barbie on the other side of him. We were watching the sun go down as the Aurelia churned through the water on its way to India.

Three days had passed, which was long enough for all the patients to be treated and released from quarantine. Everyone on board had been given either the cure to treat their symptoms or the vaccine to stop them getting sick and the anchor was finally raised just a few hours ago.

Jermaine hadn't poured my drink; he was merely controlling Ramone's movements until he was strong enough to take over as my butler again. Dr Kim said it would be a few days yet but even under doctor's orders, Jermaine had been uncomfortable with Barbie and me bringing him out onto the terrace to join us.

The US Navy captured the terrorists here so quickly, they hadn't been able to contact their colleagues in Manilla which meant the SEAL team sent to rescue Dr Mendoza's family met zero opposition. With his family safe, the good doctor stayed on board to make sure everyone infected was fully recovered. He was on board still, electing to remain in case the disease wasn't fully eradicated. The poor man was wracked with guilt despite constant reassurances he was not to blame, so I guess his commitment to remain was a form of atonement.

Commander Shriver had relinquished her captaincy, but only once Alistair Huntley walked himself back onto the bridge. Still weak, he had forced himself to return to active duty, blaming himself for his deputy's failings. Her too speedy advancement hadn't equipped her for the higher office and responsibility, he said. A new deputy captain would be joining us in India where Commander Shriver would be departing the ship. Her position on board was no longer tenable it seemed.

As for the two of us, well, our romance had barely gotten started when he fell ill but under doctor's orders to take it easy, he was to join me for a quiet night in my suite shortly. Ramone would prepare a light dinner and I planned to have him sit with me to watch a movie – a safe and benign activity while his strength returned.

Soon though, when he was strong enough, I had a more strenuous and pulse-raising activity planned. One of us needed to seize the initiative so it might as well be me.

The final element to wrap up isn't... well, it isn't wrapped up yet. Max and Amy and Agnes and Mavis were in the brig. I felt sorry for them. Each had risked their lives to help out and Max had saved my life at the very end. Okay, he was trying to steal from my suite and had broken in to do it and then got trapped there when the fake Dr Chouxiang Junior also broke in, but I was still alive because of him.

There wasn't much I could say or do about their incarceration though. Rick and Akamu appeared to be smitten by the ladies and to my eyes it was mutual. They were upset about the two women facing a life behind bars and were visiting them every day. What could they be charged with though? Apart from the crimes aboard the ship, the cruise line had no interest in them and no proof they had done anything else wrong. Unless Interpol were after them, they might get off lightly.

It was something for another time, I wasn't going to be able to sway anyone's decision about it today. Though I did wonder how much influence over their fate Alistair might have.

I sighed a deep sigh and sniffed my glass of gin. Then lifted it high in a salute to my friends. 'Bottoms up.'

The End

Author Note:

As I reach the end of this book and begin to consider tackling the next, my wife is making preparations for our son's fourth birthday. We are blessed with what many consider to be a large garden, most of which I acquired when, after moving in, I discovered an untended piece of scrubland behind the house. Several years of letters, negotiations and legal fees made the land mine and thus began the laborious process of turning it into the beautiful, lush, green landscape we now have.

So, Hunter's party, with all his friends from pre-school and all their siblings and parents and maybe even grannies, will be in our garden providing the weather is kind. Typically, September in the South East of England is warm and sunny where July and August usually bring rain. I'll find out in two weeks. I doubt the children will care as my wife has prepared dinosaur themed activities for all of them.

The quest for a sibling continues, though perhaps it isn't meant to be, and I should be grateful for the perfect child I have. Whatever the future holds, I get to be one of those guys that knows how lucky he is to have the life I live and the wife I hold. I learned from my father that wanting more is an endless chase that misses the point. Unless what you want is more book from me that is. You can have more of that.

Were it not for the annoying full-time job because I need to pay the bills, I would most likely write the remaining five Patricia adventures before Christmas. I already know what happens in each of them and have maps and plans and hand-written notes ready to go. Writing in the winter months is harder, forcing myself from my bed at 0500hrs to write is less appealing not least because the heating is not yet on at that time of day. Determined to transition into a life as a full-time novelist though, I must continue to fight the good fight and acknowledge how privileged I am to be able to do it.

Thank you for reading this far. I hope it goes without saying that you are the one that gives life to my characters. They exist only when you read them and play out the scenes I describe in your head. I thank you for that and promise to have more for you soon.

If you click over to the next page, you'll find an extract of the first chapter of the next book in this series. **Murder on the Dancefloor** will see Patricia, Jermaine, Barbie, and others embroiled in mystery again as the Aurelia plays host to India's version of Dancing with the Stars.

This is not my first series though; there are many other books already waiting for you. So, if you enjoy Patricia's adventures, you may wish to check out **Tempest Michaels**, **Amanda Harper** and **Jane Butterworth**. Like Patricia, they solve mysteries and their stories are written to make you laugh and keep you turning pages when you really ought to be going to sleep.

Finally, there is a **Patricia Fisher** story that you may not yet have found. It is part of this series but sits apart from it. It is called **Killer Cocktail** and you can have it for free. Just click the link below and tell me where to send it.

[Yes! Send me my FREE Patricia Fisher story!](#)

The Missing Sapphire of Zangrabar
The Kidnapped Bride
The Director's Cut
The Couple in Cabin 2124
Doctor Death
Murder on the Dancefloor
Mission for the Maharaja
A Sleuth and her Dachshund in Athens
The Maltese Parrot
No Place Like Home

Extract from Murder on the Dancefloor

Clues

'Madam, you have a spot of paint on you.' Jermaine emerged from his adjoining cabin two seconds after Barbie and I came through the front door to my suite. Somehow he was always ready and dressed and expecting me. Of course, now I had a tiny canine alert system to tell him I was home. Anna had leapt from her position asleep on the couch the moment the door started to open. Barking her indignation at being disturbed, she calmed when she saw it was me. By then, of course Jermaine was through the kitchen and into my living space. He spotted the paint instantly.

I looked down at myself. 'Where?'

Barbie was staring too and had there been anyone watching it would have looked as if the three of us were examining my boobs. 'Just here, madam.' He pointed to himself to indicate where I should look. 'Perhaps looking in the mirror will help.'

I moved a few feet to the full-length mirror by the entrance lobby. There was indeed a blob of paint on my dress. It was right under my left breast and thus impossible for me to see without a mirror. The paint was a bright yellow but only the size of a fingertip. 'It's dry,' I said as I scratched at it. 'It wasn't there when I put it on.'

'Where did you find wet paint?' asked Barbie.

'I have no idea,' I said with a grumpy sigh. The dress, which had not been cheap, was ruined most likely. I doubted the mark would come out. I tried licking a finger and rubbing it. 'It's not water soluble either.'

Jermaine stood back and fell into his relaxed butler's pose where he waited for instruction. 'I wasn't expecting you back so soon, madam. Was the show not to your liking?'

Barbie answered him, 'There's been a murder.'

His eyes flared in surprise. 'Another one?'

'They are getting to be a habit,' I conceded. 'I'm going to change.' With a final tut at my ruined dress, I began undoing the zip at the side and stomped across the carpet to my bedroom. I could hear Barbie filling Jermaine in on the little we already knew as I stripped off my dress and looked in my wardrobe for something else. Would I go back to the ballroom? It still surprised me that the show hadn't been interrupted but I might need to go back in so I selected another ballgown from the rack, thankful that I had more than one that fitted me.

Then, I spotted it, my heart freezing and a cold shudder zipping up my spine as I spun around to stare.

On my nightstand was a little white calling card. 'Jermaine!' I shouted, my legs feeling weak from shock. I could hear feet running, my butler ditching decorum for speed as he raced to see what urgent need I had.

He and Barbie burst into my bedroom seconds later, Jermaine instantly stopping and turning about. 'Madam, you need a gown.'

Oops. In my shock, it hadn't registered that all I had on was my knickers; the ballgown didn't allow for a bra to be worn underneath. Barbie grabbed a robe from the ensuite bathroom. 'Patty, what is it? What made you shout? I half expected to find another body in here.'

I pointed to the nightstand. 'That's the same calling card the murdered girl had impaled onto her chest with a kitchen knife.'

Barbie gasped and Jermaine hung his head. 'Someone was in the suite and I didn't hear them,' he said, his voice full of shame.

I touched his arm, trying to impart that he could protect the suite from all invaders. 'Have you been out?'

He lifted his head. 'Yes. I went to the crew gym. I was out for almost an hour indulging myself when I should have been protecting the suite.'

'Nonsense, Jermaine. You cannot be here every second of every day. I want to know what this is about though. These cards have been popping up for weeks, exclusively in the top deck suites but nothing has ever been taken. We need to check now and see if we can find anything out of place or missing. Then we need to tell security, this could affect their investigation.'

'Very good, madam.' He about turned and went back into the suites main living area where he began to check cupboards and cabinets. There were several expensive objects in the suite; oil paintings on the walls and other items such as vases in locked glass display cabinets.

'We should check the safe,' suggested Barbie. I quickly zipped up my dress and crouched to examine the calling card. I didn't touch it, and I didn't know what I was looking for, but it was evidence of something and that made it important. It confused me that the same card was impaled on the knife that killed Dayita. She had been on the ship for barely more than a day but the calling cards started appearing long before that. Were the two connected or not?

'We should check the safe,' Barbie said again, breaking my concentration.

I stood up. 'Yes, we should. Let's do that now.'

We found Jermaine back out in the living area. He was over by the kitchen and looking through the draws there. 'I cannot find anything out of place, madam. Whoever was in here to leave that card, doesn't seem to have taken anything.'

'It's so strange,' I muttered. Anna pawed at my foot. She followed me around only when she wanted something and seemed quite independent the rest of the time. Usually, when she made a point of getting my attention, she wanted a biscuit. It was probably the case this time, but as I glanced down at her, I caught sight of something. Staring down at the carpet, I called for my butler, 'Jermaine, can you look at something over here please?'

Moving at his glacial butler's pace once more, he crossed the room. Next to me, Barbie had followed my gaze but she couldn't see what I was seeing. 'Is Anna okay?' she asked, wondering if I was concerned about my dog.

I pointed to the carpet. 'Can you see the four indentations?' I moved my finger around to show them all four. 'And the dust over there?' I pointed to a line of dust.

'I'll have that cleared up in a jiffy, madam.'

'No, Jermaine. This is a clue. I think. I saw the same marks and line of dust on the carpet in Irani Patel's room earlier. When Barbie and I came passed his room earlier, he was arguing with Deepa Bhukari about having touched her, but I noticed on the floor by his feet, four odd little indentations in a perfect rectangle. See how it looks like something heavy was here and now it isn't?'

Barbie and Jermaine both nodded. That was what it looked like. In the carpet near my safe were four small indentations like the feet of a table would leave behind if it sat in the same spot for a time and was then moved.

'What could have made it?' asked Barbie.

It was a question that had me stumped and what the line of dust meant I had no idea. 'Can you take some photographs with your phone?' I asked her before turning to Jermaine. 'Do we have a tape measure somewhere? I want to compare this to the one in Mr Patel's room.'

'Of course, madam.'

While Jermaine fetched a measure and Barbie clicked pictures with her phone, I opened the safe. It was hidden behind a large oil painting that hinged out from one side. I didn't have much in there because I am a woman of limited means. It was a point I should probably start worrying about as I have no income once I return home to England in a few more weeks, but I did have a reserve of cash I was hoarding to tie me over. The cash came as an insurance payout from recovering the sapphire but I would need it to set myself up in a new home. I felt a minor flutter of worry that the safe might be empty when I opened the door, but it wasn't. The cash, my passport and a few other items were just as they had been last time I looked.

'What is this person's motive?' I asked myself. When Barbie looked at me I started talking. 'They break in to the suites on the top deck where most of the guests are very rich people but they don't take anything. They risk being caught each time they enter someone else's cabin but they have been doing it for weeks. They even leave a calling card as if bragging that they cannot be caught.'

'What about the murder?' Barbie asked. 'Do you think maybe Dayita disturbed the person and he or she killed her to protect their identity?'

I shrugged. 'If she disturbed someone in her room, surely she would have been killed in her room. Also, the celebrities are all staying in suites, but I don't think the professional dancers are. If this calling card criminal only breaks in to suites, then he couldn't have bumped into Dayita.'

'Unless she was in someone else's suite,' said Jermaine.

That put a new spin in things. 'If she was involved with one of the celebrities then that could easily be the case,' I thought about that for a second. 'Who would it be? Taginda said she was sleeping with Rajesh, Taginda's dance partner, but also said he was gay though he instantly denied it.

Barbie looked at Jermaine. 'You've got a good nose for this. If you met Rajesh would you be able to tell if he is gay or not.'

'That depends,' my tall butler replied. 'If he is still hiding it, it is far harder to know to any degree of accuracy.'

I walked across to the desk and the computer there. 'The question really, is whether Dayita was also sleeping with one of the celebrities and if so which one? Can you find out which cabin she was staying in. There may be clues there and I want to check that the four indentations don't appear in her room.'

As Jermaine slid in front of the computer, I continued to think about what I had seen at the show. 'Barbie, did you notice how late Irani Patel was to arrive this evening?'

'Yeah. The show almost started without him.' We locked eyes, both thinking the same thing at the same time. 'He did come across as a bit of perv this afternoon when he grabbed Deepa.'

It fit. It was a bit of stretch but it fit. 'All the dancers were lined up to dance so none of them could have killed Dayita. The judges were in their seats, but the host was missing and no one seemed to know where he was.'

'And he looked sweaty like he had been doing something strenuous,' Barbie added. 'Do you think it could be him?'

'It could be anyone. Or, more accurately, it could be lots of people. He has to be on the list of suspects though.' Then there was the pregnancy test. I told them both about that and what it could mean. If Dayita was pregnant and having an affair with Irani, had he killed her to escape the scandal? I grabbed my phone. 'We are going to need reinforcements.'

Made in the USA
Monee, IL
27 July 2021

74364339R00095